NINTH GRADE BLUES

BRUCE INGRAM

SECANT
PUBLISHING

For information about this title, contact the publisher:
Secant Publishing, LLC
P.O. Box 79
Salisbury, MD 21802
www.secantpublishing.com

ISBN 978-1-944962-34-0 (paperback)

Library of Congress Control Number: 2017935536

Printed in the United States of America

Dedication

Many thanks to my Lord Botetourt High School Creative Writing II-IV students who read, proofread, and commented on this book.

Sophie Barranco
Alexis Bowman
Jake Bryant
Heather Finley
Krysten Fitzgerald
Hunter Graham
Evan Grey
Alex Heck
Nikki Jani
Noah Jarrett
Jessica Lancenese
Grayson Palmer
Daphne Spangler
Dillon Switzer

Many thanks also for my Creative Writing I students who did the same

Maddie Deskins
Madison Gunther
McKayla Hoke
Mikayla Micek
Logan Olson

And thanks also to school staff members who read and commented on the book

Kendel Lively, librarian
Tim Wimer, English teacher

FIRST
SEMESTER

Week One

Chapter One: Luke

I hate the first day of school. I hate school. Yesterday evening after supper, I did what I always do the last evening of summer vacation…ride my bike around the neighborhood. I felt so melancholic (that's a vocabulary word I learned last year in eighth grade meaning *gloomy*). Yep, that's me…melancholic. I'm pretty much that way all the time, I don't know why.

Maybe I do. I'm 14 and nothing good seems like it's ever going to happen to me. Take for instance, sports. I've tried most of the usual sports except football. At 5'7" and 135, no football coach is going to take a look at me. One hit from one of those 250-pound seniors and I'd be down for the count, anyway—just a tackle dummy during practices.

I've played rec league baseball the past three years, and I did okay…well, okay, the first two years. I started at first base all three years and hit about .275 the first two years. But most of the guys got a lot bigger their eighth grade year and I barely grew at all. That third year my average was .185 and all four of the hits I had all season were infield singles. I couldn't hit the curveballs at all and most of the time the pitchers just blew their fastballs right past me. When I would make weak contact, I would dribble the ball somewhere in the infield.

That's how I got all my hits…weak groundballs and beating the throw to first. Now, I can run fast all right. I never got thrown out trying to steal. I once stole home in a game. That's the biggest thrill I've ever had playing sports. I felt cocky on the base paths, knowing no catcher could ever throw me out. I think that's the only reason the coaches started me, thinking that if I lucked out getting on base, it was as good as a double. And if the next batter hit so much as a blooper into the outfield, I was long gone across home plate. I played first base because I couldn't throw a baseball worth anything—I broke both arms when I was a kid and that will take away the old arm strength. I wasn't what you would call a five-tool baseball player. I was a two-tool one. Running and fielding was about all I can do. I sure couldn't hit for average or power, or throw well.

Basketball wasn't my sport, either. I may be fast but I'm not quick, and there's not much call for 5'7" shooting guards who can't handle the ball well and can't get off their shots against taller players. Last year on my middle school's eighth grade team, I scored two points the entire year…which is about right when you're the third string shooting guard. I think I'm done with baseball, basketball, and football except for pickup games with other guys who can't play any better than I can. Maybe I'll try tennis…maybe I'll try track. That could be my sport, I don't know.

My mom wants me to go to college. She says I've got potential. She says I'm a very good writer; that she loved to read the stories I would write when I was a kid. I still write those stories, but I never show them to her anymore. I bet she knows I still write them, but I always tear them up as soon as I finish them.

I'm an only child. I don't know why I don't have brothers or sisters; Mom and Dad seem to get along really well. Dad and I don't get along. He yells at me all the time, like when I'm mowing the lawn. He says I don't keep the lines straight when I'm mowing the grass, that I keep missing spots. I try, but all we have to mow with is a big, heavy push mower and sometimes I think it's pushing me around instead of the other way around.

I think Dad is so angry all the time because he works all the time. He works third shift, midnight to 8 A.M. at the plant and it's hard, physical labor. Then he comes home and runs his used car business from our house. We've always got four or five old cars at the house that he is fixing up to sell. He'll sell a couple, then buy a couple more clunkers and fix them up and sell them too. He makes me wash those cars and is always yelling that I leave streaks all over the place. He's right; I do, I'm not tall enough to reach across the top of the car, and my attitude is bad anyway, because I know he's going to yell at me no matter how hard I try.

After he works on the cars, he tries to get some sleep for a few hours. When I was little and I would accidentally wake him up in the afternoon, he would run down the steps, yelling, and then cut a switch from our forsythia bush. And whip me four or five times across the legs. I'll never have a forsythia bush in my yard when I grow up.

Dad doesn't want me to go to college. He said he only made it through eighth grade and things turned out okay for him. Mom finished high school, but her family didn't have the money to send her to college. She and Dad got married right after she graduated anyway. Dad was already working at the plant. He's worked himself up from being a window washer to an assistant floor manager, whatever that is. I'll say this for him…he's a hard worker.

I don't see how I can go to college when I hated grade school and middle school so much. Maybe high school won't be so bad when I get there today.

Chapter Two: Elly

I like school, and I can't wait for the first day back, especially English, history, and math classes...just about everything except health and gym. You see, I gained six or seven pounds in both the seventh and eighth grade, and I was a little heavy before that. I don't want people looking at my chubby legs in those short little gym shorts.

I don't like to play the sports we play, especially basketball and softball, in gym class, either. I can't dribble a basketball and some of the taller, more athletic girls are always stealing the ball from me, and I feel like they smirk after they do. It's so embarrassing. Softball's just as bad. I can't hit that stupid ball, and I always play the outfield when my team is not batting. I try to sort of hide out there, but somehow the ball always seems to find me, and then I have to run after it, and I just feel like the other girls are saying, "There goes old chubby legs chug, chug, chugging after the ball."

Then come the showers, and I feel like the other girls are staring at me all over again. I have frizzy brown hair and it frizzes up even worse when it's wet. The gym teachers never give us enough time to work on our hair after we finish playing those stupid sports. And then I've got to go to my next class and my frizzed hair is all clumped together, and I look worse than usual. Once I put on my glasses, which make me look like a half-blind mouse, everybody can see that I'm a dazzling beauty.

All summer my best friends Mary and Paige have been letting their hair grow out. They say the high school boys will like it longer. That must be true because when I see high school girls at the mall, most of them have long hair. But the way I see things with my hair, if I grow it out, I'll just have longer frizzy hair that's out of control. Right now, my hair just comes to the top of my shoulders. I don't know what I'm going to do about it.

I'm the oldest of three kids. My brothers Michael and David are four and six years younger than me. They don't bother me much except when they come snooping around in my room when I'm reading. But both of them can't seem to hold thoughts in their stupid, little male heads for more than three seconds, so they usually don't stay long. I love my little brothers, and just last year Mom and Dad started paying me to let me babysit them when they go out to dinner.

I love my parents. Daddy's a manager at the telephone company, and he gets these fantastic deals on cell phones. As soon as some new phone technology comes out, Mom, Dad, and I get new phones—it's great. I guess we're what you call middle class. Our house is nice and Dad pays somebody to mow our lawn, and every summer we go on a couple of vacations, usually to the beach and a state park. Mom doesn't have to work, but she has plenty to do around the house and with her sewing group and church. I don't mind helping her clean up around the house.

I want to start dating this year, even if it's just some boy having his parents drop us off at the mall or at a movie. Or maybe my parents will let Mary, Paige, and me meet some boys at the mall or at the movies. Dad hasn't said whether I can go out with boys this year. I worry that no guy will want to go out with a frizzy-haired, chubby-legged girl wearing mousy glasses. So Dad doesn't have too much to worry about.

I'm going to college. My parents have already started saving money for me to go. I think I want to become a teacher. I like little kids, and I want to do something with my life that is meaningful. I think I would like helping little kids learn how to read and write. I could see these little second and third graders coming to me for help and I'm showing them something new or how to add or subtract or something like that. Then those kids start smiling at me and I go home feeling good about myself and my day and feeling that I'm doing something meaningful with my life.

And I see myself coming home to a big house in the suburbs with definitely a husband and maybe two kids waiting for me. My husband will be tall with dark hair and kind and good looking. He'll be a businessman like Dad or maybe a doctor or lawyer or something like that. We'll have enough money to do things, but we won't be wasteful or snobbish.

Our church wedding would have been perfect, not too big or small, and Mary and Paige would have been my maids of honor. The three of us talk all the time about what type of guys we're going to marry and what we are going to do for a living and what type of house we're going to live in. I want to find someone to love me, but I know I don't really know what real love is. I'm too young for a serious relationship this year, but I would like to have a boyfriend if Dad will allow it. I worry that probably no guys at school will be interested in me.

I've been studying my school schedule. It says I have first period English 9 Honors with Ms. Hawk. Mary and Paige are in the same class and they say that they heard that this is Ms. Hawk's first year of teaching. I love to read books, especially romance novels, so I hope she will have something interesting for us to read.

I hope Ms. Hawk has got it together. I hate those classes when those young female teachers let the boys get all out of control. Boys my age are so immature. I want to date at least a tenth grader this year. A junior would be even better.

Chapter Three: Marcus

Well, today is the first day of school, but I've already been back a month because of football practice. I'm a freshman on varsity. That's pretty impressive if you ask me. I have to be honest, I thought Coach Dell was going to ask me to be on the team after the season I had last year in middle school. I ran a 4.8 in the 40-yard dash, and I was the starting wideout. My favorite play is the end around. Once I juke my way past the linebackers, the next stop is the end zone. Not even the corners can keep up with me. And the safeties are trailing way behind.

I'm planning on getting a college scholarship to a D-I school like Alabama or one of the other SEC schools or maybe a Big 10 school. I think I can be ready for the NFL after my third year in college, but if it takes four I can handle that. I'm 6-foot already and my brother Joshua is a junior and 6'4" and the starting tight end on the team. So I see myself being at least as tall as him.

I really look up to Joshua. He's got a smoking hot girlfriend, Jordan, who's also a junior. Joshua said that we could double date some this year with the first time being Homecoming in October. I haven't been on any dates yet, but Mom and Dad said I could this year if I get a girlfriend.

That shouldn't be too hard. I've got a half dozen girls already hitting on me, smiling and flirting and flipping their hair. Jordan told Joshua that some of the ninth graders in her neighborhood are already asking if I've got a girlfriend. Look, I know I sound cocky, but I've worked long and hard to get to where I am. I ran sprints and distance all summer and then I cooled down by lifting. I feel really good about myself and how I look and feel.

Mom and Dad said they would buy me a car after I pass my driver's license test next year. They said that was only fair because they gave Joshua one when he was a sophomore. Dad runs an insurance agency and Mom makes good money as a real estate agent, so we're doing okay. Joshua got a new car when he started driving, so I think I will deserve one, too. I don't want some four- or five-year-old piece of junk to drive around girls and my friends in. That would be embarrassing.

The house we're living in now was one that Mom was going to try to sell, but she thought it was perfect for us and we bought it. It's on five acres with a pool and an indoor tennis court. The setup is great for Mom and Dad throwing parties, and they said Joshua could have a party this fall if he wants to. But with both of us on the varsity football team, and chances are that we will be going to regionals, Joshua thinks we may have to wait until wintertime to throw a big bash. That makes sense.

My schedule says I've got Ms. Hawk for first period English 9 Honors, then math, history, lunch, biology, art, and gym. Coach Dell fixes it so that his players have easy classes the last two periods in case we have to travel to a Friday game.

I've always done pretty good in school, I usually get a *B* or a *C* in all the core classes and ace the elective stuff. I just want my grades to be good enough that when I get offered a D-I football scholarship, no coach is going to have any concerns over my grades. I don't really have a favorite class, and I don't have to do much studying to make good grades. Just listen when the teacher thinks she's talking about something important, then cram the night before a big test. It's a good system.

I'm going to major in sports medicine or sports journalism or something like that in college. I'd like to go into TV or work for ESPN when my pro football career is done. I could see myself being a color commentator or something like that. They hire a lot of ex-players for those jobs.

I like to dress sharp. I like it that Coach Dell requires his players to wear a nice shirt and tie on game days and wear a blazer on road trips. I think the girls like to see us looking sharp, not decked out in steel-toe boots and a camo shirt like those redneck country boys did in middle school. They look even more ridiculous when they wear their hunting jackets during deer season. I bet their fashion sense won't have improved when they hit high school.

They're not my competition for girls or sports or anything else anyway. I don't have any competition. I'm competing against myself to get bigger, stronger, and faster this year. It's like Joshua says—when you can walk the walk and talk the talk and look the part, you're not bragging. You're telling it the way it is. It's going to be a great year.

Chapter Four: Mia

I feel a lot of pressure about school starting today, but I'm confident I can handle it. I made an A in every subject every year in middle school. The pressure comes from my parents; their parents were immigrants, and Mama and Poppa never let me forget that or our Hispanic heritage. They say I have to make an A in every subject to prove that we belong here. That I have to be valedictorian. That I have to get a scholarship. I know that I belong here, that we belong here, and I don't feel that I have to be the top student in my class...just one of the best ones. I have faith in myself, that I will get a scholarship

My grandparents were illegals, but both my parents were born here. Poppa works on a construction crew and Mama is a nurse at the hospital. Poppa has a part-time job there on weekends that Mama found out about and he applied and got it. I really admire my mama and want to be like her. She worked her way through nursing school, and now has this really neat job and she says the doctor is really great to work for. She and the doctor work with little kids.

We've moved a lot over the years, but now we live in the best place we've ever had. It's got a really nice backyard where Mama and I can have a flower garden and raise vegetables and have chickens. Mama knows everything about plants and she's teaching me. We grow tomatoes, squash, beans, gourds...all kinds of neat stuff. Mama has the prettiest flower garden in the neighborhood!

I don't know exactly what I want to do with my life. Mama and Poppa want me to be a teacher, and I could see me doing that. Mama likes being a nurse so much, maybe I could be a doctor. That would take a lot of money and a lot of years, but I could do it. I really think I could. I like science, I like English and history and art and health, everything except gym.

Poppa already has told me that I can't date this year. He said he'll have to wait and see if I can go out my sophomore year. He said there were some nice Hispanic guys at the middle school, and those boys will be at the high school this year. That I should look them over. I could see myself going for a Hispanic boy, but I could also see going out with a white boy or a black one and there will be some Asian boys at school, too, like there were in middle school. I think a lot about the type of boy I want to marry, and I want him to be nice and treat me right and make me feel safe. And I want us both to have nice jobs and get really situated in a nice house and a nice community before we start having kids.

Poppa and Mama are very religious, and we go to mass every Sunday, and sometimes during the week. I think we go too much. I know it's important, but I always have so much school work to do and chores around the house and yard that sometime I feel stressed and I don't have time to do everything. I'm not sure I'd have time to date this year anyway.

Poppa and Mama want me to get a part-time job next year, maybe working no more than two evenings after school...nothing that would interfere with my schooling or grades. I could save that money for college. They said they could pick me up after school let out, that I could get some of my school work done while I was waiting for them to get there with our car. Then one of them could come pick me up from work after it was over, and I could eat after I got home. I think all that could work. My parents are really good about making things work out.

I watch how they go about deciding things. Poppa acts like he is in charge, but I notice that he usually never makes a final decision until Mama tells him what she thinks. And lots of times, it seems like she is the one making the final decision. I want my husband and me to be partners, and I told Mama that one time. She smiled and nodded. Mama and I talk all the time. A lot of my girl talk is with Mama. We talk almost every night after we put Isabella and Emma to bed. They're six and eight. I want to be the type of mother to my kids that Mama is to my sisters and me.

I talk a lot with Camila and Hannah, too. We've been best friends since my family moved here part way through sixth grade. We've already checked our schedules and we're in some classes together. We're all in first period English 9 Honors and in second period French. It would be a joke if I took Spanish. I guess English is my favorite class. I like to read novels and plays, some poetry if it's about love and feelings. I like to write, but not that boring type writing that we have to do for the state tests. I like to write about how I feel about stories and life and the world. What stories mean or something that I can give my opinion on. I can hardly wait for the day to begin.

Chapter Five: Luke

Crap, this is worse than I thought it would be—much worse. Ms. Hawk has arranged all the desks in a circle so that we can "interact with each other" and her. And everyone can see each other when we discuss things. I don't want to discuss things. I don't want people making fun of my opinions. I never raise my hand in class. I always try to sit in the last seat of the last row, the desk that is nearest to the window at the back of the room. The only break that I got was that when I came into the room, there was a seat empty next to Allen. He's my best friend. His dad takes us fishing at least once, maybe twice every spring. My dad says he's too busy to take me.

I don't want to interact with anybody except Allen. All I want is to be able to look out the window and dream about going fishing or being out in the woods wandering up into the mountains and seeing stuff or being anywhere except here or working with Dad. Crap, crap, crap.

Class starts out just awful. Ms. Hawk, I can't stand her already, says that she wants everybody to introduce themselves and tell something about them. And what they want to be when they finish school. This makes me so nervous that I can't think, and I don't listen to anything anybody else is saying. So I can't copy what someone else has said when it's my turn. Then all of a sudden she's asking me what my name is and I mumble it out and start to say something sarcastic like my goal in life is to learn what is the youngest age somebody can be to drop out of school. But just when I'm about to say that, I get worried that that is the type of smart remark that's going to get me sent to the assistant principal's office in the first five minutes of the first day of school. The secretary will call home. Dad will answer and get mad because he's been taken away from his cars, and I'll get punished when I get home. So I stutter out that I don't know yet and freeze up. I think Ms. Hawk can tell that I'm humiliated, so she hurries on to Allen.

Then I get mad at myself. I'm not stupid. I like to read, but not those dumb school stories and poems. Every day in middle school after I gulped down my lunch, I'd get a pass to the library and go read the sports section of the newspaper and the fishing and hunting magazines, then go online and read some more stuff about the outdoors and sports. Every time I come across a new word, I look it up or figure out what it means. Then I use those new words in my stories. I hope I can get a pass here to the library every day.

Ms. Hawk passes out the literature books, and I'm thankful that we're not going to do those stupid grammar worksheets first thing. I know how to use commas, I know how to write. That's the one thing I am good at. She says we're going to study the 1930s the first thing and read the short story, "A Christmas Memory," about a boy growing up then. Then read a book called *To Kill a Mockingbird* and everybody will present PowerPoints on historical stuff from the decade. Why can't we read a book like *To Kill a Deer* or to *To Catch a Bass*? And that PowerPoint crap has got to mean that I'm going to have to stand up in front of the room and tell stuff to the whole class. Oh crap.

To my big surprise, the short story is interesting from the start. I'm absolutely shocked. It's about this country boy growing up in this shack with his girl cousin who is very old and has mental issues. And they go out into the woods and creeks and do things with their dog. I can see myself in the boy.

Ms. Hawk starts out doing all the reading, then says everybody is going to read two or three paragraphs. And she calls on me first…no, no, no, no, please no.

Maybe she thinks I'm too stupid to be in honors English because the way I answered the what are you going to do with your life question and is going to weed me out of the class early. She's going to send me with a folded, stapled note to guidance, I know what that means. I've been sent down a level in math classes. So I take a deep breath, get my nerves together, and read three paragraphs. I don't make a single mistake and don't mispronounce a single word. I'll show her I belong here. Then she asks what the word *dilapidated* means and can anyone tell from the context and what does the word *context* mean. I figure that I don't need to raise my hand because I'm the one that's been reading, so I say that context means figuring out what a word means from the way it's used in a sentence and that *dilapidated* means old and worn out like the shack those people are living in. It's the first time I've ever answered in school without the teacher calling on me.

Ms. Hawk then tells me next time to raise my hand before speaking and then she smiles at me, actually smiles, not in a laughing, making fun of way of smiling, but smiling because I gave the right answers. And then she says great answers and moves on to the next person to read. So in the first ten minutes of the first class of the first day, I've kept my temper under control so that I wasn't sent to the assistant principal and showed the teacher I wasn't stupid so I wasn't sent to guidance for a schedule change. Is this what having a good day in school means…not being sent to two places you didn't want to go?

The next person starts to read, but I tune him out. I'm in a hurry to find out how the story ends, so I read ahead. The boy has all kinds of issues and gets sent away to a military school-type place like Dad threatens to do to me all the time, but I know he won't because we don't have the money to do that.

And the story ends with two kites symbolically flying away into the sky. The story is absolutely great and while I'm still thinking about those symbolic kites, the rest of the class finishes the story and Ms. Hawk tells us we have to write a 300-word paper on what those kites mean. Then she gives out the PowerPoint topics and mine is the Night of the Broken Glass from November in 1938. I can write the paper, no sweat, but the thought of giving that PowerPoint to the class makes my stomach churn up into knots.

Chapter Six: Elly

I was going to wear my skinny jeans on the first day back, but then I decide that's a bad choice with my legs the size they are. I can't make up my mind what to wear instead so at 7, I text both Mary and Paige. They're already up and dressed and working on their makeup but they have time to help me. My wearing a skirt or dress is absolutely out, what with the weight I gained over the summer. My other pair of school jeans are a little tight, too, and I don't want anybody to see the outline of my chubby thighs when I sit down. So I decide on a nice long loose-fitting dark brown blouse that Mom and I bought when we went back to school shopping last week, pulled over capris. The dark brown blouse has the benefit of not making my dark brown frizzy hair stand out, too. I look worse than usual this morning.

When I go early to first period English, I'm surprised to find the chairs in a circle, but I like that…it's different and hopefully fun. Mary and Paige soon come in and sit on both sides of me. I hope Ms. Hawk keeps the seating chart this way all year. I'm really glad that I didn't wear a dress or jeans to class now; nobody's going to be able to see how big my chubby legs are.

Right before the bell rings, I look around the room and count how many boys and girls there are…fourteen girls and eight boys. Oh great, there are only eight guys, and I'm not likely to be noticed by any of them with all the pretty girls in here. The lack of boys is just like it was in middle school when there were a lot more girls than guys in the honors classes, especially the English and history ones. The math classes were about equally divided. They say guys are better than girls at math. Maybe that's true, but I like math.

Ms. Hawk asks us to introduce ourselves and when my turn comes I say I think I want to be a grade school teacher, that I think I would like working with little kids. Mary says she wants to go into business for herself and Paige says she wants to be a social worker. I can see that. A lot of the boys' answers are so dumb, do they not have a clue what they are going to do? Grow up! Marcus says he is going to be a pro football player. Oh, right, what are the odds of that. And then his best friend Caleb says that he wants to be an NFL quarterback, which is even dumber to say. I'll give them one thing, they're both super good looking. I hear they're both going to start on the varsity, which is pretty impressive.

We finally get started and Ms. Hawk starts to read. She is sitting in our circle with her legs crossed and most of the guys are staring at her legs instead of listening to her. She probably shouldn't have worn such a short skirt the first day of school, especially the way we are sitting. I bet she'll figure that out. Then she calls on Luke to read our first story of the year, "A Christmas Memory," and I can tell he's uncomfortable by the way he fidgets when Ms. Hawk calls on him. I've been in the same classes with him all through school, and I bet we haven't said ten words to each other. He's smarter than he thinks he is, and he's kind of cute. His best friend Allen reads next, he's tall, blonde, and good looking. I'd break my tall, dark, and handsome rule for him in a second. But Allen would never ask me out.

Ms. Hawk calls on me to read, and I try to pronounce every word correctly and with expression. I want to make a good first impression and show her I can be a class leader. I like the story a lot, and I like the PowerPoint assignment that comes next about events in the 1930s. All the topics look interesting: mine is how the Holocaust got started. We've got to write a paper about "A Christmas Memory" due tomorrow and complete the PowerPoint in one week. I can't wait to get started.

Algebra I is next, and many of the same kids are in that class. That's the only bad thing about being in honors' classes, you're basically with the same kids all day. But I'm also with Mary and Paige most of the day, and we have the same lunch period. Mrs. Haley is the Algebra teacher, and we spend most of the period reviewing what we learned in eighth grade. I like math but it's not exciting like English and history are.

Nothing much happens in World History I third period except the teacher goes over the course outline for the whole semester and ends the teaching part early to talk to some of the football players. But Mary, Paige, and I get to do some serious talking in lunch. We decide to rate all eight of the boys in first period from first to last on who we would like to go out with. Allen comes in first in all of our lists. He and Caleb are the best looking by far. Caleb is more than a little stuck up but he still comes in second in all our lists. Really all of our lists are about the same except I have Luke in third, and Mary and Paige both laugh at that and Mary calls him a ragamuffin for the way he dresses and ranks him last, and Paige agrees. I start to defend my choice, but then I realize they're both probably right. But later I think, you never know…sometimes those quiet, shy boys might surprise you.

Chapter Seven: Marcus

Ms. Hawk is one super-hot woman! When she walks across the room in that short skirt, I can see that I'm going to like English just fine. The first thing she asks us to do is tell what we want to do with our lives, and when it's my turn I say play professional football. I can tell she's really impressed because she smiles like she is agreeing with me. My best buddy Caleb goes next, and he says he wants to play QB in the NFL. We've got to be one of the best freshman QB and wide receiver duos in the country. How many schools in the country have two future NFL players starting as freshmen. That's why Caleb and I both think we're going to win state this year.

Then we start reading this story about some backwoods hillbilly in the dark ages. Just once I'd like to read some stories about black guys playing sports, but that's like impossible I guess. But I have to tell you I spend most of the reading time scoping out the females and admiring Ms. Hawk's legs. There are only two black girls, Jayla and Kylee, and both of them are hotties, but Jayla has already shot me down several times. Kylee might find this to be her lucky year. But I'm an equal opportunity employer, female-wise, so who knows who might get to be on my arm around Homecoming time.

We finish reading the stupid story and Ms. Hawk assigns us a huge 300-word paper on the symbolism. Doesn't she know I've got practice after school and a big game on Friday. I can tell you what the symbolism is…a dumb, hillbilly kid gets sent to reform school because he's a dumb hillbilly kid—end of story. I'll work on my paper Wednesday night; practices don't last as long as they do on Mondays and Tuesdays because we've already put our offense in by then. I like some of the PowerPoint topics. When it's my turn I choose Jesse Owens. I know he stuck it to Hitler in the 1930s, and I want to know more about him.

Algebra I is next, and it's a snap. I usually make a *B* in any math classes I take, and I never study and even don't always do all my homework. Math has always come easy to me. World History I is my third period class, and Mr. Foster, our quarterback and receiver coach, is the teacher. I bet Mr. Dell arranged that. Coach Foster stops teaching with about 10 minutes to go. Anyway he calls Caleb and me up to his desk, along with Micah the backup tight end to my brother. Coach Foster says he drew up some really neat plays for Micah and me and the other receivers and tight ends and wants to show them to us. While we're up there, I look up just for a second and spot Kylee watching me. I smile, and she looks away, but I may just have to pay her a visit during lunch one day.

And that day is today—her lucky day. She's sitting next to Jayla, and I come up to their table and just sit myself down and start talking and turning on the charm. But I don't stay long because I tell them I've got some more people to see. Joshua always says leave the ladies when they're still wanting more, that's what makes them go for you. He really understands women.

The afternoon classes aren't worth talking about. I keep looking at those plays from Coach Foster and studying over them. Finally, it's time for practice, and Coach Dell gives us a long pep talk before we start. He says this week is when practice really starts and it's crucial that everybody be on the same page before our first game on Friday night. Joshua told me Coach would say something like that. Joshua said crunch time would really start when we played our last two regular season games against Northwood and King, both on the road. Those two teams beat us bad last year, but last year Caleb and I were setting middle school records. Things will be different now—the reinforcements have come!

Put it down right now that Caleb will be good for four touchdown passes this Friday night and at least two of them will be to me. And we'll just be getting warmed up on what we can do. By those last two games, we will be unstoppable, and the whole school will be talking about us. I'm ready to dominate.

Chapter Eight: Mia

I'm almost late for school on the first day. Our car won't start, and I have to wake up and cook for Isabella and Emma while Mama and Poppa are trying to decide what to do about the car and who they are going to call if Poppa can't fix it, and how they are going to get to work. I wanted to wash my long, black hair—it comes down to my waist—but there's no time for that now, and by the time I get my sisters on their bus and me on mine, I haven't even had time to comb it. I didn't even have time to gather eggs from our henhouse. It's a good thing I set out all my clothes to wear last night.

I finally get a chance to catch my breath when I get to first period English Honors. I feel like my hair is greasy and messy, and Mama still won't let me wear makeup. I know almost everybody in class. Elly smiles at me when she comes in and Paige waves. The chairs are arranged in a circle and all the boys clump up next to each other, just like they did in middle school. They are so immature; it's like they're afraid of us or something.

Ms. Hawk seems really nice. She starts the class talking about her basic rules, and I write them all down. Then she says she is going to start reading "A Christmas Memory," and each of us is going to read in turn. I love the expression in her voice and when my turn comes, I try to read just like she did. I love the story, I can relate to the little boy in it…not because the adults in the story are cruel to him…my parents are wonderful…but because he feels out of place. If things were like they were in middle school, there will probably be only about twenty Hispanic kids at this school, and some of them aren't as well off as my family is. And I know that some of the students in middle school looked down on us. Every day, I'm going to work hard to show that I belong here, that we belong in this country.

After we finish reading, Ms. Hawk gives us a paper to do on the short story and says it is due tomorrow. I love to write and I love the assignment about analyzing the symbolism. I'll start on it as soon as I get home. Then she says we are going to do PowerPoints on historical events in the 1930s, shows us her PowerPoint instructions and rules on her website, and the topics. I'm impressed that she already has all of our names on little scratch sheets of paper, and she has Mary draw names from a bucket to see who gets to go first. When my name is drawn, I choose Philo Farnsworth, the inventor of the television. I'll work on that after I take care of the chickens and help Mama cook dinner.

My next class is French I, and the first thing the teacher Mrs. Aldridge does is give us out a list of twenty vocabulary words to learn by Friday for a quiz. I already can figure out what all of them mean, what with my Spanish background and Mama making sure from the beginning that I could speak proper English and know all the grammar rules. French is going to be really easy.

Then I go to honors World History I, and most of the same kids from first period are in the class. I see a seat open next to Luke, and I go sit next to him. He is so cute, but he doesn't know that he is...do you know what I mean? He is so shy. Last year, we were in the same vocabulary study group in English 8. When the teacher assigned the words, he and I were the only ones that knew all of them. We didn't even bother to look them up, it was so cool. Luke never talks in class unless the teacher calls on him. I didn't know he was so smart before that day last year.

I know Poppa probably won't let me date this year, and I don't know how he would feel about me going out with a white boy, but I'm going to try to spend some time this year working on Luke…trying to get to know him better and showing him that I like him. He may be too shy to get the hint, though…lots of boys are like that, or at least they were in middle school.

Camila and Hannah and I had all planned to meet at lunch and go over our day, but I was a little late getting there. The first thing Hannah says is that she got a text saying I walked by and talked with Luke a little bit, is that why I was late? That news surely spread fast. What's up with that, she giggles? I try to play it off and change the subject, but they both are having so much fun with it, that I just let it ride. Sooner or later, they'll make a play for some boy and then it will be my turn to analyze all that boy's little flaws in front of them.

I don't have a cell phone; Poppa says they are too expensive and I'm too young, maybe next year when I get a part-time job and can pay for it myself, and he will have to be called to pick me up from work. I must be one of the few kids in school that don't, but I understand why. We're not poor; we're not lower class. But we don't have money to throw around, either. I'm going to succeed and have a good life, I just know it. I have a bright future, all my teachers last year told me that.

Week Two

Chapter Nine: Luke

I checked my grades online when I got back to school on Monday. I've got a middle *C* in English, an *F* in math, a low *B* in history and a low *C* in everything else…so things are going about like they usually do. I got an *A* on my symbolism paper on "A Christmas Memory." Ms. Hawk wrote all these compliments all over my paper, it made me feel good. But I got a low *C* on my PowerPoint and a 0 on a homework worksheet on sentence diagramming.

The PowerPoint thing started off bad and just got worse. When we got to the computer lab, Ms. Hawk told Elly and me that we needed to coordinate our PowerPoints since she was doing hers on how the Holocaust got started and mine was on The Night of the Broken Glass. So we had to sit next to each other at the computers and work together. That made me so nervous that my stomach started churning again, and I could barely talk. Meanwhile, Elly was smiling the whole time and chatting away with me about what she was finding out about the Holocaust.

I've got a confession to make. I've had a crush on Elly since the eighth grade. Every time she would see me, she would smile, and she's still like that in high school. I know she's friendly to everybody, it's not just me. But that's why I like her. She's smart, too, and pretty, and she has the most beautiful green eyes and long eyelashes, and gorgeous curly hair, and she doesn't put people and their ideas down when we have class discussions. The whole working-together thing should have been a way for her to learn that I'm somebody worth knowing and that I'm not stupid. Instead, I blew it. The truth is I'm not ready to go out on a date with Elly or any other girl this year. How can I when I can't even have a conversation with a girl, and my stomach is always feeling like it's about to explode when I try to. I worry that Elly is out of my league anyway, even when I am older.

When I presented my PowerPoint to the class last Thursday, I just mumbled and rushed through it and didn't "expound" on any of the bullet points like Ms. Hawk told us we had to do. At the end of class when I was walking out, Ms. Hawk called me to her desk and gave me one of those teacher pep talks. She said she gave me an *A* on my PowerPoint creation, but an *F* on my presentation, for an overall grade of *C*. She told me to try to relax, that she could tell I was tense all the time, but that I had good skills. I appreciate her trying to make me feel better, but she doesn't know how hard standing in front of the room is for me. Then her voice turned sharp and she started in on me on why I didn't do the homework worksheet on sentence diagramming, that learning how to diagram sentences is the key to learning how to write better, that she wanted to know why I had not done the assignment and she was waiting for an answer.

Then I said did she want to know the truth, and she said yes, and I said that I thought I was a good writer, that was about the only thing in school that I was any good at, that I had never been able to figure out sentence diagramming, that it made me think of math, and that I thought that diagramming sentences was stupid and confusing and had nothing to do with being a good writer. It was the longest conversation that I've ever had with a teacher. She got this shocked look on her face, and then I was scared to death she was mad at me. That she thought I was being smart-mouthed with her, and so I apologized for speaking that way. For a teacher, she's not bad. And then Ms. Hawk said the strangest thing...that I had given her something to think about. Then she gave me an excused tardy to remedial math class, which I milked for everything it was worth, so I was five minutes late coming to class, which was just about the high point of my week in math. Everybody in there is as dumb as I am and most of them are guys. There are only three girls in the whole class and it seems like there must be 50 people in there but I know there are not. It only seems like it because most of the guys act up the entire time and it's just crazy—inmates running the asylum-type crazy. That's all I've got to say about that awful class. That's all I want to say about the whole awful first week of school.

I had an awesome weekend. Mom and especially Dad are big NASCAR fans, and this year they said that I didn't have to go with them to the races, as long as Granddaddy would come over or call and check in on me. I hate going to the races with all the smell and noise and not having time during the weekend to go off into the woods by myself and walking and exploring or fishing in the river. Dad knows somebody at NASCAR who is in charge of programs, so he gets some and sells them in the stands before he settles down with Mom and watches the race. Dad always says he makes enough money selling programs to more than make up for the cost of going to a race. Dad is always hustling to make money, he's good at it.

I spent Saturday in the national forest. It's about three or four miles from our house, and I ran all the way there. I run three miles before school every morning. I love getting up early in the dark and running when nobody is around and listening to the night sounds and looking at the stars. After I got to the national forest, I got on my favorite trail and hiked till about noon, then ate a couple of peanut butter and jelly sandwiches from my backpack, drank some water, and headed back.

Granddaddy got me tree and bird field guides last Christmas because I asked him to, and I'm trying to learn how to identify every species of songbird and tree that I come across. Saturday, I finally figured out the difference between scarlet oaks and pin oaks and that we have scarlet oaks here. I heard or saw about twenty-five species of birds when I was up in the mountains, including this American redstart…the first one I've ever seen. It was awesome.

Sunday morning, I rode my bike to the river. I tucked my two-piece rod (that I asked Granddaddy to get for me the Christmas when I was nine) under my arm and put my best lures in a creel over my shoulder. I caught this huge 15-inch smallmouth bass on a Rapala minnow and a 14-incher on a Cordell Big O crankbait. That's good fishing, really good fishing. I'm going back to the mountains and the river next weekend, especially if Dad and Mom go to the races again.

I hope this week in school is not as bad as last one. Fat chance of that happening.

Chapter Ten: Elly

I had a fantastic first week in school, a really fun time at the football game Friday night with Mary and Paige, and I can't wait for the second week to start. Friday afternoon when I got home from school and I had given the teachers enough time to type the grades for the week into their computers, I went online and checked. And I had an A in everything!

Mary and Paige and I had decided at the start of the week that if we didn't all get dates for the football game Friday night that we would all go together. Both Mary's and Paige's parents have said they could date this year, but my dad still hasn't made up his mind. I think he hopes that this whole dating thing will just go away or that no boy will ask me out at least this year. But I've got to have an answer ready if some guy does ask me, that is, a guy that I would like to go out with. Then I start stressing all over again that nobody will want to go with a chubby-legged, frizzed-up hair, old lady glasses-wearing girl like me.

When I ask Mom if I'll ever be pretty, she always says, "There's always somebody for everyone." What's that supposed to mean...that there's always a guy dork for every dorky girl? I know Mom doesn't mean for what she says to be an insult, but it sure sounds like one. I need to at least get some contacts and lose 10 pounds.

Paige said she thought Allen was going to ask her out on Wednesday and again on Thursday, but it was like he couldn't make up his mind on what to say or do, or how to go about asking and finally on Thursday after coming up to our lunch table and sitting down and talking for five minutes, he just got up and left and said he hoped to see us at the game Friday night. Ninth grade boys…well, what can you say.

Mom says it's wrong for young girls to ask boys out, and I sort of agree, and Mary, Paige, and I have debates all the time about when we do start dating, should we ever ask out a guy. Mary says girls should never ask out a guy for the first date, but after they've been dating for a couple of months, it's okay for a girl to make suggestions on where to go. Paige says that we can get them to ask us out by "flirting like an expert," but that didn't work out so well for her on Wednesday and Thursday with Allen. She was smiling and nodding to everything he said and laughing at his silly jokes, and he still didn't take the hint.

I really like the book that we're reading in English, *To Kill a Mockingbird*. I can really relate to Scout. All around her she can see stupidity and racial prejudice, and none of it makes any sense to her. One day when we were discussing the homework reading assignment, Ms. Hawk said she was going to go around the room and ask everybody which character they could relate to and why. I think what she was really trying to do was to see if the boys had been reading the homework chapters.

When Ms. Hawk got to me, I said that, besides Scout dealing with stupidity and racial prejudice, I liked how she walked away from a fight with Cecil Jacobs because her daddy said that was the right thing to do. That I liked characters that tried to do the right thing. Some of the other students' comments were really interesting. Mia said she could relate to Calpurnia the maid because her grandmother was a maid and had to work hard all her life for other people's children in other people's houses. That her grandmother said she never had time to take care of her own family and she was too exhausted when she got home to do hardly anything and she felt guilty about that. Mia said that she bets Calpurnia feels the same way. I know that there are kids at this school who feel that every Hispanic kid here is an illegal, but Mia must be the smartest person in the freshman class. I'd like to get to know her better this year.

Later, Ms. Hawk asked Marcus which character he could relate to, and he said none of them, that he didn't like stories that had the *N* word in them. I respect what he said, but I was really impressed when Jayla interrupted and said that everybody needed to know what the old days were like, especially black kids whose ancestors had suffered so much and white kids who didn't know anything about those days. Jayla said that she has it pretty good now, but that her grandparents sure didn't. I really liked what Jayla said, but I could tell Marcus didn't.

The person who gave the strangest answer was Luke. He said the person he could relate to the most was Walter Cunningham, this poor, little boy who won't accept a quarter from the teacher so he can have lunch to eat and is like only in two chapters in the whole book so far. Luke said that his ancestors were poor, country people like Walter's family, that his granddaddy said that some people treated them like poor white trash, just like some people in the book treated Walter. Marcus then joked that maybe Luke's people were poor white trash, making moonshine all the time. I saw Luke's eyes flash, then he bit his lip and clammed up like Marcus had said something that had struck a nerve.

Then I remembered something Mom had told me once, that "still waters run deep," that there's more to some people than meets the eye. That I should remember that before I started judging people. I feel like I've been going to school with Luke my whole life, but I really don't know him.

Chapter Eleven: Marcus

Well, we dominated Friday night in the first game of the season, and I scored two touchdowns and Caleb threw four touchdowns just like I predicted. We won big time, 28-20…the score was not as close as it looks because they tacked on a lucky touchdown late in the game. We've got another home game this Friday, and I aim for Caleb and me to do our part. I figure I'm going to be good for at least two touchdown receptions again, and if the coach will let me do a couple of end arounds, there's no telling how many TDs I might score. When we were on defense, I looked up in the stands to see if I could spot Kylee, and I finally did. That's good that she was there, cheering me on. I'm going to ask her out real soon. I'm going to wait for just the right moment…one more big time game performance like I had Friday and that should be enough. There's an old baseball saying that "chicks dig the long ball." High school girls have got to love the long touchdown bombs and the guys that catch them—that's me.

Ms. Hawk didn't treat me right last week. She gave me a 0 on that totally stupid story on that country boy and his old woman cousin…how ridiculous is that. I mean both the story and the assignment. We got to class on the second day of school, and she said for everyone to turn in their papers. I told her that I had long practices on Mondays and Tuesdays, and I'd get the paper to her by Thursday, Friday at the latest. And she said nope, it was due today, that she had told everybody it was due today (she didn't, I didn't hear her say nothing like that) and she was sorry but my grade was a 0. That next time I should be better prepared and organized with my homework.

When I got home from practice, I told Mom and Dad that they needed to call Ms. Hawk, and Mom asked why and I told them about my unfair treatment and that I didn't deserve a 0. Mom then went online to the school's website, hunted down Ms. Hawk's website and said that the assignment was clearly listed as being due on Tuesday, that she was not calling Ms. Hawk, and that I needed to take responsibility for my actions. I said that that one paper had given me an *F* for the whole week, and that it was unfair. Then all of a sudden Dad, who hadn't said a word the whole time, got really angry and told me to stop arguing with my mother, to stop whining like a kid, that the 0 was fair and to "suck it up," and to go to my room and work on this week's assignments and think about acting like a man instead of a spoiled punk.

They don't get it...they just don't get it.

Joshua drives me home from practice every day, and one day I told him that Coach Dell needs to put in more deep routes for me, that I'm not getting enough plays called for me. Then he ripped into me, just like Dad did on Tuesday. I asked him what was his problem, and he got so mad that he pulled the car over to the side of the road and started getting in my face. He said that the basis of a good game plan was a balanced offensive attack, that everybody knew that (or should know that), that he was sick and tired of my complaining at home and at practice, and that he was embarrassed sometimes to be my brother. That I had probably more ability than anyone on the team, but that my attitude sucked and some of the juniors and seniors had complained to him about my attitude.

I said I didn't believe that anybody had complained, that everybody knew I was their meal ticket to the state playoffs and that him being my brother was probably his ticket to going to a

D-I school. That some coach would probably recruit him just to get an edge for possibly getting me to come to the college a couple years later.

Then Joshua said something to me that I couldn't freaking believe my ears. He said he had finally come to the realization that he didn't have the skills to go to a D-I school. That he had asked Coach Dell to give him an honest answer about what his upside potentially was, and Coach Dell had said that he thought my brother might could get a D-II offer, that he was a step slow and too light to play at the D-I level. That he was a fine high school player and an excellent teammate, but that wasn't enough to make it in D-I. That thousands and thousands of good high school players were making solid contributions all over the country, but that very few of them would go D-I and even fewer go pro.

I can't believe Joshua's attitude, it's like he's given up on pro football. It seems like everybody I was around last week had a negative attitude.

Chapter Twelve: Mia

My first week in high school couldn't have gone better, and I can't wait for this week to start. I babysat Friday night, Saturday, and Sunday for some families in our neighborhood, and I made really good money. Ever since I started babysitting in the eighth grade, I've saved almost all the money I've earned. I've put close to $500 in the bank. I figure that once I start working part-time in tenth grade and if Mama and Poppa let me work after school and on weekends when I'm a junior and senior, I should be able to save quite a bit of money for college. Then if I can get a full scholarship, or at least part of one, I can go to college somewhere. I'm going to college no matter what; Mama and Poppa both want me to. I won't let them down.

My campaign to get to know Luke better had a real break-through. I noticed that the first couple of days, he gulped down either a peanut butter sandwich or a couple of hot dogs, then walked over to the teacher on cafeteria duty and got a pass to leave. We can get a pass to go to guidance, the bathroom, or the library, so I figured the library was where he was going. So Thursday, I got a pass, walked to the library, and found him reading online.

I smiled and sat down next to him, and he gave me a nervous smile back, but that's just Luke. I asked him what he was reading, and he said that he was reading about the Jewish and Palestinian issue. That he usually came to the library to read about sports and the outdoors, but he had gotten interested in the problems of the Jews when he was working on his PowerPoint on the Night of the Broken Glass. I knew there was more to Luke than meets the eye. How many kids are going to give up socializing time in the cafeteria to come read in the library about historical or current events. But maybe he's just so shy that he's miserable in the cafeteria.

Friday, I decided to go to the library to see if I could run into him again, and this time he didn't smile so nervous-like when I sat down next to him. He wasn't at a computer station but was sitting at a table and working on math problems. He's taking remedial math, I could tell by the book cover. I knew Luke wasn't in any of my math classes in middle school or in Algebra I this year, but I didn't know that he was that low.

I asked him how he was doing in his math class and he just groaned and said his grades were awful already and that his mom had told him before school started this year that if his math grades didn't improve, she was going to get him a tutor on Saturdays. That he tried harder and worked harder in math than all of his other classes, but he always did worse in math than any other class. And that meant he wouldn't be able to go fishing on Saturdays or go hiking up in the mountains. So that's what he does on Saturdays. That probably means he doesn't have a girlfriend either.

I said I could help him with his homework if he wanted, and then he really smiled and said that would be great, that it wouldn't be cheating because it wasn't a test or anything like that. I started looking at the problems he had done so far and most of his answers were wrong and the problems were so easy. So I started giving him clues on how to fix them, and he acted so grateful and was like thanking me every couple of minutes.

I've heard that Luke's grades aren't very good, especially in math. Teachers always make this big show about how confidential the grades are, but we already pretty much know what everybody else is making. We finally finished up his math homework and correcting everything, and he was really thanking me. I said I could maybe tutor him during lunch a couple times every week, and he said that would be great and that he would find some way to thank me.

I do enjoy helping people any way I can, that's why I think I would make a good nurse or doctor. But I want to get to know Luke and for him to get to know me, and maybe our sophomore year, maybe we could date some. I hope that that's not bad for me to think that way. I feel like I would help him out, even if I wasn't interested in him.

I told Luke that he could let me know when he needed help, and then he said he didn't have a cell phone, so he couldn't text me, and then I said my family couldn't afford for me to have one either. We both laughed at that, and he sarcastically said that he and I must be the only two people in the ninth grade that didn't have cell phones. And something else hit me when he said that. I don't feel that my family is poor, we're not lower class, but we don't have any extra money either. I sort of think Luke's family is like that. There are probably a lot of white boys that wouldn't go out with me because of my family's situation, plus the Hispanic thing. But I think Luke is the type of guy who wouldn't care what somebody's social class was. I really believe that. I know a kind person when I see one.

Week Four,
Friday Night

Chapter Thirteen: Luke

Normally, Friday night is like every other night of the week for me: washing one of Dad's cars that he recently bought or doing some other car-related chore like vacuuming the insides, eating dinner with Mom since Dad's at work, doing homework, and then watching some sport on TV. Mom and Dad have never bothered giving me a curfew because I don't have anywhere to go. But Allen invited me to go to the home football game with him because his older brother Russell was taking him. Russell teaches at another district school and has coached all kinds of sports, including the baseball team that Allen and I were on last year. I don't care anything about watching high school football, but the real reason I came was that Allen invited me to spend the night at his house, so that Russell could take us fishing early the next morning. Allen said that Russell knew about this farm pond that was just full of big largemouth bass.

When we were walking to the stands to get a seat, we saw Elly, Paige, and Mary heading the same way. Allen has been telling me that he has been sort of hinting around with Paige about asking her out for a date, but he hasn't been able to get a read on how interested she might be. I told him not to expect any help from me on how to go about figuring out how interested Paige is. Who knows what girls mean when they do the things they do. So the five of us stopped to talk while Russell went on up into the stands to find us seats.

Well, I should say four of us stopped to talk. I took one look at Elly, and she smiled at me, said something about something I don't remember what, and then my stomach and nerves started fighting with each other, and the next thing I heard was Allen saying that we had better go find our seat. Did I even say anything to Elly? Allen told me later that he should have invited the girls to sit with us, but who can think of such things when the pressure is on. He's a lot smoother with girls than I am, but he's got a ways to go. Inviting the girls to sit with us would never have occurred to me. But it sure would have been great to have sat next to Elly and gotten to know her better. I don't know what I would have said to her, though. Maybe she would have done all the talking. Girls are good at doing most of the talking, I know that much.

While we were waiting for the game to begin, Russell asked me if I was going to try out in the spring for the high school baseball team. I told him no, that I was done with baseball. To my absolute shock, he told me I could make the team, though I would probably never be a starter all four years. I wouldn't mind riding the pines, just getting to play in practice would be enough for me. Then I asked him why he thought I could make the team, given my .185 batting average last year.

"Why do you think you batted leadoff," he said. "Your on-base percentage was probably close to .500 with all your walks and getting hit by a pitch. After you got on, you almost always stole second right away."

Russell said that I could really help the team as a pinch runner and pinch hitter, though I would very likely not get on base as much from walks or being hit since the pitchers' control would be better at the high school level. Then he said something that surprised me and made me feel really proud...that I was a good teammate and he could tell that I really studied what was going on and tried to get better.

Russell was full of surprises all night. Later, part-way through the third quarter, after Caleb and Marcus had hooked up for two long touchdown bombs, and the school was up 14-10, Russell asked Allen if Caleb and Marcus ever talked about playing college football. Allen said all the time, and Russell replied that he thought that they might could play D-I ball, but definitely D-II. Allen then got into an argument with his older brother and said both guys were aiming for the NFL. Russell guffawed (that's a vocabulary word meaning *loud laughing*) so hard that I thought he was going to have a coughing fit.

Do you realize how many high school football players, said Russell, are out there playing right now? Do you realize how many of them think they are going to be pros, do you realize what the odds are of making the NFL? Thousands and thousands to one. Allen kept arguing and said that both players were way above average, that they were high school superstars.

Russell said right back that both of them have some serious flaws. As a quarterback, Caleb has no touch, no feel for the ball or the game. He's got a very good arm, but all he wants to do is throw the long pass, that when he needs to hit Marcus or somebody else across the middle, he relies on arm strength instead of touch. The result is a ball that often comes in too fast to the receiver, or either too high or too low or behind the player, said Russell.

If all Caleb needs to do to complete the pass is dump it off to a back coming out the backfield, he zips it into too fast even when the guy is wide open or hesitates when he should just throw a touch pass. Russell really lit into Caleb for his attitude toward his offensive linemen. All three times that Caleb was sacked, we could see him yelling like forever at his linesmen when he should have been getting ready for the next play. Just as bad, said Russell, was Caleb later began to get happy feet when he was under pressure...throwing the ball too soon before the receiver had run his complete route.

Next, Russell starting criticizing Marcus as being too soft, that Russell had recognized a definite tendency for Marcus to hesitate when he was called to run his routes across the middle—that he was afraid of getting hit. That Marcus also didn't understand how to use his height and size to get in between a player and the ball and that when Marcus was not the hot receiver on a play that he had a tendency to half run his routes. Marcus is pretty good at catching the long ball and he has very good speed, said Russell, which should make him a lock for II, possibly I. Caleb should be able to make a II squad somewhere, said Russell.

The real test, the real crisis for Caleb and Marcus, said Russell, would be how they reacted when the bitter truth hit them…when they finally realized as juniors or seniors that their NFL dreams were hopeless. Would they be men enough to understand that life goes on after high school, especially if it's a life different from what they thought it was going to be? We won the game 28-21 to make us 4-0 for the season, but Russell said just wait until the team played its last two games on the road…that the team was going to get stomped.

Chapter Fourteen: Elly

"The best thing about going to football games is watching guys with awesome butts running around in tight pants." That's the first thing Mary said after her parents dropped off her, Paige, and me at the football game. Homecoming is next Saturday night, and Mary said the second best thing about coming to the game was that it was the perfect time to scope out guys who showed up without some girl on their arm.

The first thing on Mary's agenda was to linger around near the stands until Allen arrived, so that Paige would maybe have a chance to flirt a little bit. Allen had told Paige, during one of his almost daily stops at our lunch table, that his older brother Russell was taking him to the game on Friday night. So we waited and waited and finally Allen and Russell showed up.

I was surprised to see that Luke was with them. He just doesn't seem to be the type to want to go to a high school football game…he's such a nature boy and all. When Allen walked over to us to say hi, Paige really turned on the charm. She moved in a little closer to him, smiling big-time, then tapped him on the shoulder saying what an awesome looking cobalt blue, long-sleeved shirt he was wearing. Meanwhile, I guess, to make the moment linger so that Paige would have time to work her "magic," Mary struck up a conversation with Russell, asking him where he worked, who did he think would win the game, and wasn't this fall weather fantastic. Paige's act was so obvious, but what else was she going to do. She's been talking to Allen for weeks, but she hasn't gotten through to him.

So I was left in the position of having to talk to Luke. I think Luke is a really good person, but he's not much of a conversationalist. I asked him who he thought was going to win the game tonight, and he just sort of shrugged, and then I told him I was surprised to see him at the football game…that didn't seem to be his thing. Then he mumbled something about spending the night at Allen's house and going fishing the next morning. Well, that makes sense. Luke decided to suffer through going to a football game, so he could go fishing the next day. If any girl ever dated Luke, she'd probably have to go fishing and canoeing and hiking and all kinds of outdoor junk with him. I can't see myself ever wanting to go out on those kinds of dates…bugs, snakes, and no bathrooms…yuck. But still…there's something appealing about Luke's sweetness and shyness. He'd need the right kind of girl to bring him out more, though.

It was getting closer and closer to kick-off. Luke and I had run out of things to say. Well, I had run out of things, Luke didn't have much to say obviously; and Paige and Mary were still yapping with Allen and Russell when Paige played what I thought was a brilliant trump card. She said she had worn a skirt that was too short to the game (sensibly, I had worn a pair of baggy jeans that served the twin purposes of keeping my legs warmer and hiding their chubbiness) and she saw that Allen was carrying a jacket for when the night turned colder and maybe did he have an extra jacket or blanket or something in the car that she could borrow…just for the night?

This turn in the conversation caused Allen to take a quick glance at Paige's legs and mini-skirt (it was very short) and hopefully put some thoughts in his stupid male brain to invite Paige and us to sit with them and let her wear his jacket to keep her arms warm. (She knew, all of us girls knew, that no guy had enough sense to bring along an extra jacket or a blanket period…good grief.) I wish I could think of things like that when talking with guys. But all Allen said was that he was sorry, that that jacket was the only one he had. He should have at least offered his jacket to Paige, then he would have had to meet up with us at the end of the game and that would have given Paige another chance to work her charm. I bet that was her backup part of the plan…seeing him after the game in order to return the jacket…in her scheme to spend time with Allen and convince him to ask her out.

Finally, Allen said they had to go get to their seats, so the guys left. Paige was absolutely beside herself with frustration, and I can understand why. Honestly, I was relieved that Allen didn't invite us to sit with them. It would have been a long, awkward night trying to make conversation with Luke, but, still, maybe I wouldn't mind much getting to know him better…if he would only open up a little.

The whole first half we didn't watch any of the game, I have no idea what was happening and really, I don't care anything about football anyway. We spent all that time analyzing everything Paige did and Allen said, and what did he mean by this or that and was he really that clueless about Paige being interested in him, or maybe he had already asked some other girl out to Homecoming and who would that girl be if he had. And Paige wanted to know over and over if Mary and I had seen Allen talking to any other girls, and we had to keep reassuring her over and over that we hadn't. It was exhausting.

Anyway at halftime, Paige got this text, and it was from Allen, and he'd asked her out for Homecoming! The first thing I thought was finally…the second was that texting isn't a very romantic way to ask somebody out for a first date. But at least that crisis was out of the way. When I got home, I told Mom that Paige was going to Homecoming with Allen … just sort of seeing what would be her reaction and maybe she would ask if some guy had asked me out. But, no, all she said was that Daddy and she had decided that I was too young to date this year. Actually, I was relieved at that…nobody would want to go out with me anyway. The way I look. I've got to lose some weight and figure out how to deal with my hair, maybe a really short cut?

Chapter Fifteen: Marcus

The game started out just awesome. First possession, Caleb hooked up with me on a post pattern, then a stop and go…I gained 35 yards in just two plays. Then for some stupid reason, Coach Dell called three straight running plays…what's up with that foolishness. We barely got a first down off of those running plays. I mean, like two minutes into the game, and I'm dominant and I've got the other team already on the ropes.

Then Coach Dell wised up and called for me to run a route across the middle, but Caleb threw the ball behind me and it was almost intercepted. A draw play came next, for like four yards…just another wasted play. It was third and six, and Coach Dell finally got smart and called an end around for me. The other team was in their prevent defense, the linebackers bit on that it's a pass play when Caleb dropped back…he handed it to me…and all of a sudden I zoomed around the left side and it was hello end zone for me from 52 yards out! The crowd just went wild. I looked for Kylee up in the stands to see if I could find her. I reminded myself to tell her all about my moves when we double date with Joshua and Jordan after the game. Yep, it's going to be an awesome first date with the hottest girl in the freshman class.

The other team ground out a touchdown on their first possession; it was like an eight-minute drive and our defense couldn't stop a single third down play. But when we got the ball back, I dominated again. First play, Coach Dell called for a fade pattern, and, man, I made that cornerback look silly...23 yards worth of silly in fact. Then Joshua got his number called for the first time all night, and he went across the middle for a 12-yard catch and run. Two more wasted running plays picked up all of six yards, and then Caleb hit Joshua for five yards across the middle again...first down.

We're on around the midfield marker, and Coach Dell came to his senses and called for the bomb. Caleb threw it too short, the cornerback and me both go up for the ball...like you know who's going to come up with the football in a jump ball situation. We got our feet all tangled up, the corner fell, I caught the ball and righted myself and boom, I was gone. Like, the second quarter had barely started and I'd already scored two TDs.

The other team made a field goal their next possession, and nobody scored again before halftime. Caleb kept messing up with his passes. By then, the other team had put a corner and a safety on me every pass play...well, duh...and Caleb kept throwing it too long or too short. And for some reason, Coach Dell forgot all about that I can't be stopped on an end around, and he hadn't called it again. At halftime, I told Coach Dell that I needed the ball more, and he gave me this long, angry stare and told me to go hydrate. I swear, we should have been ahead of this team by three touchdowns by halftime...they've got no game, especially their defense.

The second half didn't start off well. Caleb got sacked on third down three straight possessions...our offensive line sucks...and by the end of the third quarter Caleb was screaming at them. I mean those guys are juniors and seniors...haven't they learned how to block yet. It was still 14-10 at the end of the third quarter, and Caleb really let Paul, our junior center, have it on the sideline, telling him that if he couldn't block any better than that, he was going to tell Coach Dell to put somebody else in. Then Paul got up in Caleb's face and shoved him, and some of the guys had to get in between them. Our defense, which hadn't done much all night, then intercepted the ball and one of the corners went in for a score. We're up 21-10, but the other team went right in for a score on the next possession and then, to everybody's surprise, went for a two-point conversion to make it 21-18. Then Caleb tried to hook up with me across the middle, and, man, he threw it behind me again, and they intercepted it and ended up kicking a field goal and the score was tied.

Okay, tied score and we're down to two minutes left in the game and we take over just short of midfield. Like, who do you think needs to get the ball. We got into our two-minute drill and Caleb hit Joshua on two straight dump offs, and we were down to the 35. A draw play to the halfback got us five yards closer to pay dirt, and it was my time to shine. Coach Dell called for a hitch play to me, I grabbed the football at the 20, slanted away from the safety and outran the corner to the end zone and that was that. My first three touchdown game, and I send the crowd home happy.

After the game, Joshua and Jordan and Kylee and me went out for pizza, and I could tell the girls were impressed with their menfolk. Joshua and me were way too tired to do much more than chow down on pizza, and by then, it was nearly 11 anyway and Kylee has a curfew. After we dropped off the girls, Joshua lit into me about my trying to tell Coach Dell his business during halftime. And that I had better tell my good buddy Caleb that he needs an attitude adjustment or Joshua was going to do it for me...and it won't be pretty. Man, we won the game because of Caleb and me. Big brother, lay off.

Chapter Sixteen: Mia

I had so much to do after school Friday. First, it was time to put the garden to bed for the fall because we've already had two light frosts, and the next one was going to finish off our tomato plants which were already looking thin and droopy. So I picked all the tomatoes that were left and most of them were green. Mama and I are going to make some chili with them, and they're great fried, too. Then, I had to gather eggs and clean out the henhouse. The manure just piles up if I don't clean the coop every week, and the poop sometimes gets into the nest boxes…the hens just track it in there…and then I have to clean off the eggs before I put them in the refrigerator. Poppa just loves some kind of egg dish and spicy sausage several times a week for breakfast.

Then it was time for me to help Mama with dinner. We made this great baked fish meal with yellow onions, peppers, and garlic from the garden with roasted chili peppers and the last of the ripe tomatoes. I barely had time to help Mama clean up the kitchen, before I had to walk to go babysit a neighbor's kids. I try to make money babysitting every Friday and Saturday nights. I have four or five families that know I'm reliable and will take good care of their kids. I've saved every dollar I've made for college. I know the money I make from my babysitting and whatever my other jobs are in high school won't be enough to pay for my tuition freshman year. But it will be a start.

Friday night, I babysat the two Harmon girls; they're four and six and are pretty well behaved. I put them to bed by 8, which meant I finally had some time to myself for the first time all day. All week, Camila and Hannah, all they could talk about was Homecoming and would anybody ask them out. I know Poppa won't let me date this year, but I wouldn't have gone if someone had asked me out. I've just got to save my money for college and I'm not going to waste it on a dress for just one night. Some of the girls are going to go to Homecoming in a group, which is probably what Camila and Hannah will end up doing. But I don't want to go sit in a group of girls and hope some boy will pick me out to dance with. It would be so humiliating to not be chosen all night.

When Camila and Hannah weren't talking about Homecoming, they were teasing me about Luke. Luke and I sort of have his math tutoring schedule all worked out now. After eating a quick lunch with Camia and Hannah on Tuesdays and Thursdays, I go to the library to meet him at a table. We go over his homework for the night, and I try to help him get prepared for his weekly Friday math test or quiz. Since I've started working with him, his grade has gone from an *F* to a middle *D* and his parents haven't gotten him a tutor so far, which he says means he can still go off into the woods and outdoors on Saturdays and Sundays. I would love for him to ask me to come along, but I can't ask him to…maybe he will ask me sometime.

On Fridays, I skip lunch and go straight from third period to the library and meet up with Luke. That's our day for just sitting at side-by-side computers and reading about whatever one of us suggests. That's my favorite time of the week, in or out of school. A lot of the time we read about something that went on in honors history class, which we have together; sometimes we read about something about the outdoors. Luke always suggests that, of course. I was amazed at first about how much he knew about biology stuff. He knows all about trees, and birds and fish and what wild foods you can eat. Yet he has a D in science class fourth period. I bet he knows more about those types of things than Mrs. Burkhead does, and she's really smart. He says all she wants to teach about is amoebas and one-celled creatures and how boring is that. And then I tell him that she's got to teach the boring stuff because of the state testing and before we can get to the interesting lessons. But he's right, though, science class is pretty boring most every day, but I still have an A in it. I'm trying to convince Luke that he and I should form a two-person book club, that on Fridays we could select a book to read over the next week…that one week I could select a book for the two of us, then the next week he could. But he's been resistant to that idea.

I think a lot about Luke and wonder if he thinks of me. That's mostly what I did Friday night when I finally had some time to myself. I hope he thinks of me sometimes. But I do see him changing some. He's not as nervous in some of the classes, like English and history, as he was when the year first started. But I can imagine that he's just an all-out mess in math, and I can tell without him telling me that he can't stand Mrs. Burkhead.

I finally put Luke out of mind for a while and started reading ahead on the history chapters. Sooner or later school is going to get really busy, and I want to be prepared. Around 10:30, the Harmons got back and since they were late, they gave me an extra few dollars, plus a $5 tip. It took me 10 minutes to walk home, and I went straight to bed. I was exhausted.

End of First Nine Weeks

Chapter Seventeen: Luke

Well, the first nine weeks ended and I had a low B in both English and history, a middle D in both honors science and remedial math and a C in everything else. My grades were better than usual in English but worse in science...one of the reasons was I got in trouble on the science field trip and in class before that. Mrs. Burkhead and I have issues.

Several weeks ago, I got really excited when she said we were going on a Friday field trip to the river and take water samples and other stuff. I actually raised my hand in class and told her I could take my fishing rod if she wanted and catch fish and identify them for the other students and then we could seine up some minnows, crayfish, and hellgrammites and other creatures, and I could tell the class about the river's food chain. That sort of stuff, well, it's freaking awesome...I told her that. She said no, that we wouldn't be studying the aquatic unit until second semester in January. But I said it would be too cold to fish and seine stuff in January, and everybody could wear old clothes and tennis shoes, and we could all make seines, and I could identify everything we seined up, and I could help her with the identifications, too, if she didn't know something.

As soon as I said that, I knew I had made a mistake and started to apologize but it was too late. Mrs. Burkhead got really mad and went to her desk drawer and got out the yellow discipline referral slips...told me to come here like I was a dog or something. I looked down at the yellow slip and checked off were "disrupting class" and "socially rude interactions." She then sent me to Mr. Caldwell, the assistant principal, and he said something like young man, why are you in here, and I told him that I was "too enthusiastic about learning." Well, that was also the wrong thing to say, and then he got mad at me, told me not to get smart with him, and tell him exactly what had gone on in class.

So I did…the whole thing. And I told Mr. Caldwell that I didn't mean to show up Mrs. Burkhead about the identification of the fish and vertebrates and invertebrates, but I knew all about those kinds of animals and it was really fascinating and then I started telling him that another great idea for a field trip would be going up into the mountains and identifying all the songbirds and trees and shrubs and did he know that the hawks were migrating now and that we could maybe even see peregrine falcons and that I knew where some old American chestnut stumps were and how they once grew everywhere but were now endangered.. That there was just so much to see and do, that science and biology were absolutely awesome but amoebas and one-celled junk were not.

When I started talking, Mr. Caldwell had this mad stare on his face, but, by the end of my rambling on and on, he was smiling and nodding his head and he chuckled, I mean the man actually chuckled, when I complained about amoebas. He then told me that he wasn't going to send me to in-school suspension, he wasn't going to call home (thank goodness for that, if he had called home and Mom wasn't home and if Dad had answered because he had been woken up, Mr. Caldwell would have gotten an earful), and that I was to choose my words more carefully in class. So he checked off "conference held" and sent me back to class.

Mrs. Burkhead got this shocked look on her face when I came back, and I could tell she was not happy that I hadn't gotten at least kicked out of class for the rest of the period. I decided the best thing to do was keep my mouth shut the rest of the class. I should never have raised my hand in the first place.

A week later we were on the field trip and the boring lecture had just barely got started (she was freaking lecturing to us on a field trip and we were having to take notes when we were outside on the river...can you believe that crap) and, I swear, all I said to Mrs. Burkhead was that I had just heard the call notes of some ruby crowned kinglets, and they were coming through the area now and would she like for me to point them out to her and the class. And she got all red in the face and yelled at me to go sit in the back of the bus until we got back to school...that I was in big trouble. I started to make a smart remark, saying something like did she have problems with ruby crowned kinglets or something, but I realized I had said too much already.

When we got back to school, Mrs. Burkhead's first order of business was to write me up (she marked the same two categories on the yellow form), and I made a return visit to Mr. Caldwell's office. He told me that I needed to choose my words more carefully when I answered in class, and I told him I had decided not to raise my hand in science class anymore and that I was pretty sure Mrs. Burkhead wouldn't be calling on me anymore. Mr. Caldwell called home, meanwhile putting the phone on speaker, and sure enough, he woke up Dad and Dad let out some choice four-letter words about him, me, and the school. I spent the rest of the day sitting in the in-school suspension room and had time to read this fantastic book (which I had in my book bag) on how to fish for black bass, so being suspended wasn't too bad except that I missed my weekly Friday library time with Mia when we read and talk about neat things. She's been really nice to me and really she's the only reason I passed math because of how she's been tutoring me.

Chapter Eighteen: Elly

I made an *A* in every subject for the nine weeks, except for a *B* in health and P.E. I saw the *B* coming because I got a *C-* on the P.E. part. I couldn't run the entire mile when we did that, couldn't hit the softball when we played ball, and couldn't find my golf ball when I hit it into the overgrown ditch that runs along the sports field. Really, if Ms. Edwards had given me a *D* for the gym and outside stuff, I wouldn't have complained. But my parents were pleased with my grades and Mom understood about the P.E. grade. She said she wasn't an athlete in high school and I'm not either.

English has become my favorite class. Right now, we're studying *The Odyssey*, and last week Ms. Hawk said she had come up with a game to help us have fun and learn our vocabulary words easier, plus get extra credit points. Well, everybody was tuned in when she said that, and then she said the game was called Bonus Points and we would compete in teams to spell, define, and use in sentences the vocabulary words from *The Odyssey*. She next said that Paige, Kylee, Caleb, and Luke would be the captains, and they had five minutes to go out into the hall and have a "sports-style draft" to choose who was on the teams. Meanwhile, the rest of us were to put four or five chairs in circles and wait to see which team we were on.

When the captains came back in, Luke walked over to Mia and me and said he had picked us, then motioned to Jayla to join us in his circle. I've never seen Luke so in to anything relating to school and so talkative about it. He has been talking more in class lately, especially in English and World History, but he has totally shut down in science. He's still really shy but not "painfully shy" like he used to be, if you know what I mean. Anyway, he told us three girls that he had made a deal with the other three captains that they could each pick the person that they wanted the most, before he picked anyone. But that when his turn came, he wanted to have three picks in a row. The other captains agreed to that, and Luke said that Paige picked Allen just like he thought she would, that, of course, Kylee picked her boyfriend Marcus, and Caleb picked a JV cheerleader, Leigh (who has really long blonde hair and wears really short skirts—I can't stand her, she's so stuck-up), which was predictable too, Luke said. I was really impressed about how he understood how the other captains would choose their teammates and I've got to confess that I was glad he chose me, though I wouldn't have minded one bit being on Caleb's team—he's the hottest boy in the freshman class. Luke then gave us this big pep talk and said he had picked the three smartest girls in the room, and that we were going to win this game "big time." He said that we were to shoot up our hands immediately when Ms. Hawk called out a vocabulary word…"be aggressive," he added.

Well, Ms. Hawk calls out the first word from *The Odyssey* word list: *baleful*, and Luke and Mia shoot their hands into the air and before you know it, Mia has spelled the word correctly and Luke says it means *evil*. Then comes *precedence*, *harangue*, and *insidious*, and Mia and Luke fall into this routine of her spelling the words and Luke giving the definitions and Jayla and I helping them construct good sentences. The game is awesome, and we absolutely dominated what Ms. Hawk says is Round One of the game. We are up by like 15 points at the end of the first round.

Then Ms. Hawk says that next is Round Two, that these words are going to be really hard from the *A* part of the dictionary, but that the words won't be on the quiz but they will count for the game. And Round II will give the teams behind us a chance to catch up. Some of the words are just unbelievably difficult to spell and define: *alopecia* and *abecedarian* for example, and the other teams start to catch up to us because the point value keeps going up every time someone misspells the word or gives the wrong definition. Then Ms. Hawk says the last two words are *aardwolf* and *ailanthus*, and Luke whispers to us he knows what they both mean, and for us to just sit tight and let the other teams guess wrong and for the points to build up, then when people start to get close to figuring out the spellings and definitions, he will step in and we will grab all the points and win the game and extra credit points.

And it happened just like Luke said it would. When the points got high for both words, Luke spelled them both right and said aardwolves were like hyenas and ailanthus was an invasive tree species from Asia. I thought how on earth did he know all that, and Ms. Hawk must have thought the same thing because that was the question she asked. And then she answered her own question. "Of course," she said, "one is an animal and the other is a plant." And those answers came from a boy who told me he got a *D* in Honors Science.

So we each win 10 extra credit points for the vocabulary quiz next Tuesday. Luke (I can't believe how he's acting so excited about school, well, at least, English) raises his hand to me and Jayla, and we both give him a high five and then he turns to Mia with his open palm, and she does the strangest thing. Instead of giving him a high five, she squeezes his hand for several seconds and has, like, this shy grin on her face. What's up with that?

Chapter Nineteen: Marcus

We come into the next to last regular season game of the year 8-0, and Caleb and me have been dominating all year. Nobody, I mean, nobody, can stop him and me. And what does Coach Dell do when we play Northwood on the road? He goes all conservative and calls three running plays to start the game, and its three and out for us. Then Northwood comes down and grinds out like this 20-play, 80-yard drive, and we're down 7-0, and I haven't even touched the ball yet.

Finally, Coach Dell wises up a little bit and calls a 7-yard slant for me across the middle, and Caleb throws the ball a little high and behind me, and Northwood's corner interferes with my route, and the refs don't call anything. I scream at the ref to get into the game, our center Paul gets in my face, and tells me to get to the huddle, and I look over to the sidelines and Coach Dell's eyes are shooting daggers at me. Next, Dell calls a deep route for me down the sidelines, but when I leave the corner in the dust and turn around to look for the ball, I see that Caleb has already been sacked. It's third and 17 and an obvious pass play, and Northwood's coach sends both safeties and a linebacker on the blitz, and Caleb gets happy feet and throws the ball way too soon to me, and I haven't even turned around to catch the pass when I see it sailing over my head.

Northwood then goes on another long touchdown drive. Our defense sucks. Our corners can't defend and our safeties can't tackle, and our tackles and guards can't get any pressure on the quarterback when he does throw, which isn't often, because their running game is so strong. We're down 14-0, and there's only seven minutes left in the half, and I still haven't caught a pass. There's got to be college scouts out in the stands, and they're not seeing how I can dominate a game.

On our second drive, Coach Dell again starts with a running play, which (and I could have predicted that) gets stuffed at the line of scrimmage. It was almost like Northwood has read our playbook. He calls a halfback draw on the next play and that makes all of two yards. My number gets called on third down, and I have to go across the middle just past the first down mark. Northwood has their best corner on me, and I see the safety sneaking up to double. I don't care, two guys can't stop me. I zip across the middle and just when the ball arrives, I leap, because it's a little high, and the safety hits me high on the shoulders and the corner crunches me in the back. All three of us are like suspended in mid-air in a hot, tangled mess, and I get my fingertips on the ball but lose it when we all crash to the ground. That's the last time our offense is on the field, because Northwood goes on another long touchdown drive and score to go up 21-0 with just 14 seconds left in the half. When we get the ball back, all Caleb can do is take a knee to end the half.

Coach Dell gives us a pep talk during the half, but I can't listen to what he is saying, I'm so mad at him and the defense and the overall play calling…just everything. Things just totally fall apart in the second half. Northwood goes up 35-0 by the end of the third quarter, and their coach benches their starters, and Coach Dell benches both Caleb and me and most of the offensive line for the fourth quarter. It's scrub time all the way around, and the final score is 42-0. I catch two freaking passes for the whole game for a total of 11 yards, and the college scouts go home without seeing what I can do.

Then when I get home that night, Mom and Dad have had a chance to look up my grades online for the first nine weeks, and they're not happy with my D in English and a C on everything else except for a B in history and in math. They complain that I should have made an A in math and history, and everything else should have been at least a B or a high C. And Dad rips into me for not keeping my temper under control and for yelling at the ref during the game. Didn't he see that stupid call or was he watching some other football game. I decide to tell him that, I was so mad. Then Dad and Mom ground me for a week, which means I have to break my date with Kylee on Saturday night because Joshua and I were going to double date. What a rotten, gosh awful night.

Chapter Twenty: Mia

I did something that maybe I shouldn't have, but I don't regret it. Mama and Poppa always tell me not to be too "forward" toward boys, but I squeezed Luke's hand in English class. We had just finished playing this new vocabulary game that Ms. Hawk created, and Luke was the captain, and I was one of the girls on his team. He picked me to be on his team! How great is that! I was hoping he would.

Well, anyway, we won the game and got 10 extra credit points for our vocab quiz next Tuesday. It's always nice to get extra credit, even though I made a high or middle *A* in all my classes the first nine weeks. The other students on Luke's team, Elly and Jayla, really helped out during the game, but Luke and I did most of the work on spelling the words and defining them correctly. So when we celebrated winning at the end of the game, Luke gave Elly and Jayla high fives, but when he held his hand for me to slap, instead I squeezed it and held on to it for just a second or two. I like him so much, he is the type of boy who has a really good heart and would treat a girl well. He got this funny look when I squeezed his hand, but then he gave me the sweetest little shy grin. It just made my heart melt.

Camila and Hannah have been teasing me non-stop about Luke, but I don't care. They say that I now spend my whole lunch period with him on Tuesdays, Thursdays, and Fridays, which is true. They tease me that Luke is a terrible dresser, and that's true, too, that I must like "fixer upper" guy projects. But then Camila said that he is "pretty cute," and then I began to think that maybe they're sort of jealous that I am spending those lunches with him. I care what they think, but I don't care...does that make sense? I just like being with him. The more time we spend together during lunches, the more he opens up, and the more relaxed he seems to be with me. I don't think he's ever talked to girls much before me.

Of course, Tuesdays and Thursdays are mostly helping Luke with his math work, but our Friday get-togethers have changed from just reading online to reading a book and discussing it. Luke finally went along with my idea for us to have a two-person book club, that on Fridays we would discuss the book that one of us had chosen for the two of us to read the week before. The deal is that I choose one book that I think he would like; then the next week, he chooses one that he thinks I would like. I just thought that if he would try reading some of the books off the college bound reading lists, that maybe that would make him want to go to college more. That maybe he would see how interesting books can be...that it's fun to learn.

So the first book I chose was *Walden*. It's about this man who goes off to live in a cabin in the woods for about a year. Luke just loved that book, he said he had no idea that it would be so good. That he could see living like the author and writing about deep thoughts and life and stuff. Luke then said that the line, "The sun is but a morning star" was one of the most interesting things he had ever read, that it made him think about the future and possibilities. This is coming from a boy who told me at the start of this year that he would probably drop out of high school like his father did. Then he said he had chosen a book that he thought I would like, *The House on Mango Street*, which is by a Hispanic woman.

It really made me feel good that Luke was thinking about and respectful about my Hispanic heritage, but by the Tuesday when we met in the library to go over his math work, I had to tell him that *Mango* was one of the worst books I had ever read, that all it was about was this stupid girl's hair and hats and it was just excruciating to read. Luke then laughed, and he said the book was the most boring thing he had ever read, so we decided right then to dump it and read something else. We went to the librarian, Mrs. Kendel, and she suggested George Orwell's *1984*, which is about this dystopia in the future. We're going to read *Animal Farm* in Ms. Hawk's class second semester, and Mrs. Kendel said reading *1984* would help us understand the other book better.

I'm hoping that Luke and I can keep getting to know each other better...that maybe next year we can start dating. I would never ask him out, but I think I can show him that I would be fun and interesting to have around...that I would make a good girlfriend. Next fall when we get back to school, I could sort of hint that it might be fun for us to go do something sometime. That wouldn't be too forward, I hope. His daddy has all these used cars at their house, Luke has told me, so he would have something to drive, and we both should get our learner's permits next year. I worry that Poppa might not like me dating a white boy, and I'm not sure how Mama would react. Luke's not a fixer upper guy, he's a boy with real potential. I really believe that.

Second Nine Weeks

Chapter Twenty-One: Luke

I've been thinking about it and thinking about it, so a couple of weeks ago I asked Granddaddy if he would take me hunting. He told me he had never hunted, and I said I knew that, but that I had taken a hunter safety class in eighth grade and passed the class (you can bet I studied for that class and aced the test). And all I needed was a licensed adult to take me hunting, and he could take a hunting safety class online, and we could go. Then Granddaddy said what are you going to hunt with, and I told him I had been thinking about that, too, and maybe he could give me my Christmas present early—a crossbow. I told him I had read online about Parker Thunderhawk crossbows, and that maybe that bow could count as both my Christmas present and my 15th birthday present for next year.

Granddaddy laughed and said he could do all that, but we still didn't have a place to go. And I told him that I ride my bike around a lot and that a neighborhood about a half mile from our house had all these houses on like five-acre lots, and there's this wooded hillside with a creek behind all those houses, and I had seen the deer coming out of the woodlot into those backyards in the evenings, and maybe some of those people would let me hunt with a crossbow in their backyards. Granddaddy laughed again and said okay, and then I said I needed one more thing and that was a popup blind to put in one of those backyards, so the deer couldn't see us or smell us so easily. Granddaddy said he would try to find one at the flea market or a used one on eBay.

Granddaddy asked had I asked my dad about all that, and I said no, that he was angry or working most of the time, and I already knew that his answer would be no. That Dad had always said no when I asked him to take me fishing, and that I was going to ask my granddaddy first about taking me hunting. Granddaddy then told me he had been meaning to have a serious talk with me for a long time and now was as good as any. He said that he did not raise Dad to be the way he is, and they had had some arguments about me. Then he asked me how much I knew about what happened with Dad when I was seven. I said I knew a little.

When I was seven, the police came to our house one night and arrested Dad. Mom was shaking, Dad was angry but he wasn't doing much talking back to the police, and I was scared. Mom has never worked except to help Dad with his cars, and Mom kept asking after the cops took Dad away where we were going to get money to pay the bills. Later, I asked Mom why the police had arrested Dad, and she said that they had accused him of being a part of a stolen car parts ring, a chop shop she called it. That my father would beat the charge in court. Dad didn't have to go to prison after the trial; he always has bragged to me that he "beat the rap," that he was too smart for the cops. So I guess that means he was guilty but the police couldn't pin the crime on him.

Granddaddy said I knew more than he thought I did, and then he asked if I knew about the family curse that the men had. I said I wasn't sure, and Granddaddy said that the men in our family had a problem with alcoholism. I told him that Mom had made me promise over and over ever since I was 12 that I would never drink alcohol, and I had promised her I wouldn't, and I never had tried it like some of the guys in school had...that I would keep that promise to Mom forever. He said that was a good promise to make, and he told me to keep it, too. Then Granddaddy teared up, and he said he had been a drunk and had only stopped drinking when I was born, that he vowed to Grandmother that I would never see him drink or drunk, and he had always kept that promise to Grandmother and me. He said Mom had made Dad stop drinking not long after they had gotten married, and that he had told her he would and he had kept that promise to Mom. I knew that Mom never allowed any alcohol in the house and that she never even used any to cook with, but I didn't know about the other stuff.

Granddaddy said "now you do," and that he would buy me the crossbow for Christmas and as my birthday present and take care of the blind...but that it was up to me to find somewhere to hunt and then he would take me hunting. I told him I would get on it right away. I wanted to ask Granddaddy if Dad was still doing illegal things, but I was afraid to...that the answer might be yes. Dad talks all the time about me dropping out after high school and working with him with the cars, but I don't want to work for him. I worry that he would do something shady, and I would get arrested along with him. If I ever find somebody to marry me and we have kids, I am never, ever going to do something illegal and have the police arrest me and have my kids see their dad hauled away.

The very next day after school, I rode my bike to the neighborhood; it's the same one where Elly lives. I stopped at her house first, and she answered the door when I rang the bell. She had this really surprised look on her face when she opened the door, then she smiled at me...that smile that she smiles to everyone. She just takes my breath away when she smiles at me. I tried not to stutter about why I was there and managed to get out that I wanted to talk to her dad. He was pretty gruff when I asked him to hunt and he said no. Then I took off and visited three more houses; the first two said no, but the third man said, sure come on over.

As soon as my crossbow comes, I'm going to practice with it every morning after I go running before school. I'm going hunting for deer with my granddaddy…how awesome is that!

Chapter Twenty-Two: Elly

The strangest thing happened the other day after school; I heard a knock on the door and went to answer it, and there stood Luke. I was absolutely blown away. The first thing I thought was has he come over to see me, was that what he was doing? And how would I feel about that if he had come over to maybe see me and flirt a little.

I'm not going to lie, the boy I think I most want to get to know better is Caleb. He lives right down the street from us, and he and his parents go to the same church that we do. Caleb is my ideal tall, dark, and handsome guy. My mom knows his mom pretty well, and Mom always says that Caleb is such a nice boy and so polite to her and would be perfect for me when I get older. I'm pretty sure Mom and Dad are going to let me date my sophomore year; mom has sort of been hinting around about that lately. But I worry that Caleb will not go for a frizzy-haired chubby legged girl like me; that all those JV cheerleaders are flirting with him all the time and how on earth is he going to notice me with all those other girls around him.

But sometimes I think that Caleb is not right for me, even if I wasn't a little overweight (Mom says I'm not overweight when I ask her, but what does she know). So then I start thinking about Luke, and the more I think about how he has changed this year, the more I think that he might be the boy I should concentrate on. Anyway, I think I might have some competition for Luke…if I did decide to sort of get to know him better.

Last Friday during lunch, I had to go to the library and renew a book for a Book Talk (we have to read a book every four weeks in Ms. Hawk's class and give an oral presentation on it), and I saw Luke and Mia sitting next to each other and reading. Mia smiled and waved to me, and I came over and they were both reading a book that said *1984* on the cover. I said I had to admit that I was a little shocked to see Luke reading something that wasn't about the outdoors, and Luke said it was a pretty good book and started talking about it. That really surprised me, too. Then Mia said she and Luke had formed a book club and were reading books from a college bound reading list or ones that Mrs. Kendel had recommended. I said that I didn't see them much in the cafeteria any more, and Luke shook his head yes and said that Mia was tutoring him on Tuesdays and Thursdays for his "math for dummies" class and "miraculously" he had a middle *D* average now. Luke then said that *1984* was "awesome and terrifying" at the same time, and said I might like it. Luke talking about reading classic, college level books; I mean, how shocking is that.

Mia then tapped Luke on the shoulder and said that he was "coming along." Did that mean coming along in his studies or coming along as in a relationship with her…or both? I really like Mia, she's one of the sweetest girls in our freshman class; she's almost as good a friend as Paige and Mary. Maybe she and Luke are about to become an item, that they're "talking." I don't think I'm jealous…maybe I am a little, though. Why do I have to overanalyze everything.

So Luke is in our living room and talking to my father…which is about as surreal a scene as anybody would ever want to imagine, and Luke asks Dad if he can bow hunt behind our house for deer. Dad answers really snappy and says no, and Luke says no problem, sir, thank you, and leaves. Later, I asked

Dad what would be wrong with Luke bow hunting behind our house, and Dad said Luke's family is trashy and his father had been in trouble with the law. But that doesn't make Luke a bad person, I said, and Dad just mumbled something and went back to reading. I need to do some more thinking about this Luke and Mia thing, and how I feel about it.

Chapter Twenty-Three: Marcus

Football season is over, we got stomped in the last game, and we didn't make the playoffs. I don't want to talk anymore about it...maybe just a little. Coach Dell has no idea how important that game against King was to Caleb and me and our college and pro future. He called boneheaded play after boneheaded play, and we got beat 35-14. Our offensive line sucks and our whole defensive line can't put any pressure on the quarterback. I play against those guys almost every day in practice, and they can't defend against Caleb and me, and they sure as heck can't defend against a team like King.

I'm glad to see a lot of those seniors move on. They've got no game and even the best of them is looking at going to a D-II school at best. There was too much arguing going in the locker room with those guys; they can't stand it when Caleb tells them what to do.

I'm playing basketball on the varsity, but I'm a little behind on learning the plays and getting in good basketball shape. It won't be long, I bet, before Coach Henson puts me in the starting lineup. All I've got to beat out is a junior who, basically, has no touch from long range. Coach Henson needs a good shooting guard who can drain it from beyond the line.

It's all over school now that Kylee and I broke up last week...it was all over school, Facebook, and Twitter, man, in like five minutes. That's good because the ladies need to know that I'm available. Things started off great with Kylee and me, but she began to complain and was real standoffish about stuff. I asked her what her problem was, and she said I should know what the problem was. How are us guys supposed to know what we're supposed to do to make things right if the stupid girls won't tell us. It's like they want us to play some stupid game like 20 Questions, just trying to figure out what they want us to do or how we're supposed to treat them.

We would argue just about every day in school between classes or during lunch about something ridiculous, usually something she thought I did or didn't do, or some silly thing that I was supposed to do but wasn't doing and things like that. And finally I told her to lay it on the line about what was bothering her. And she got all sarcastic and said did I want one thing or just three or four things or all of them. And I got real sarcastic right back and said why didn't she just give me the top five or six.

She laughed this evil laugh and said okay, that will be easy. Then she said, I was "in order" was how she started out, "immature, stuck-up, and clueless." Then she said that I didn't want to talk about anything but football, that I never asked her opinions on anything, that I was insensitive about her feelings and had unrealistic goals about the future. Kylee got really harsh next. She said that the only reason she ever went out with me in the first place was that I was so good looking and on the football team. But, boy, her mama was right about looks not being everything. I got so mad at her that I said that she was nothing but "eye candy" to me, and I could do a lot better in the "looks and personality" department. So that was that with her. I won't stay single long.

I've already been talking to some new babes as potential girlfriends. I think I've settled on Camila, you know how hot those Dominican girls can be. She's got a real chance to be my number one *jaina*. The past three days I've stopped by her table during lunch (she sits with Hannah and Mia most days) and let her see what she's been missing in the man department.

Anyway, I asked her out Monday for Friday night. She said she would have to ask her parents first, that they had said she might could do some dating this year, but they weren't all the way sure. I told her no sweat, no problem, that I needed to know by Wednesday. I told her we could go double date with Joshua and his girlfriend, maybe go out to dinner somewhere nice. She said she has a curfew of 10:00, and I said that was no problem. That's my curfew too, but I didn't see any point in telling her that.

The whole time we were talking Monday, Hannah and Mia were like hanging on every word, and I don't understand why they didn't get up and go somewhere, go get some more food or go to the restroom or something, and let Camila and me have some privacy. Girls are funny like that, it's as if they feel like they have to herd up, like they were some prey animal or something like that and the jungle is full of lions.

I'm really sure Camila is going out with me on Friday. I mean she's not going to do any better than me.

Chapter Twenty-Four: Mia

Camila and Hannah (they both live in my neighborhood) came over after school on Monday to talk about the Camila and Marcus situation…he's asked her out for Friday night. Camila and Hannah were texting back in forth in all their classes after lunch, and it was one of those times I was glad that I didn't have a cell phone. I've got to pay attention and keep all my grades at the *A* level. I spend enough time thinking about Luke and me without getting mixed up in all this drama that is constant at school.

Anyway, when Camila and Hannah arrived, I said I had to do some housework and start getting dinner ready for when Mama and Poppa got off work, and I had to help Emma with her homework because I had to work on my own after Mama and I cleaned up after dinner, but I could listen and talk with them at the same time as I did my work. Camila said she had texted her mom after lunch, and she said that Camila could go out to dinner with Marcus, providing that was the only place they went and she was home "well before 10." Hannah was all about thinking it was really cool for Marcus to ask Camila out, and said he was really cute and a sharp dresser, plus a big time athlete.

That made Camila feel really good, she said, when Hannah said that, then she asked me how I felt about Marcus. When Marcus and Kylee broke up last week, I heard her talking before English class started with Jayla. Lots of us come into

English class in the morning and study, or do homework, or just chill out or to eat some fast food breakfast. I just want to be super organized before school starts and sometimes I'll talk to Ms. Hawk a little about what we've been reading. Anyway, I heard Kylee tell Jayla that Marcus was super immature and conceited, plus he was a "first-class jerk," and, really, that about sums up how I feel about him.

But Camila is one of my two best friends, and how am I supposed to tell her that a guy who just asked her out for what would be her first date is not right for her. I felt like she had really put me on the spot. So I started hedging about how I didn't know what she should do and asked her what did she think?

She said the usual things about Marcus being so good looking and athletic…blah, blah, blah. And his parents have a really nice house and all that, and Marcus says he's going to play pro football—give me a break. Then I said but what did she think about Marcus as a person? And she hesitated on her answer, and I thought maybe that I should just smile and not say anything more. Mama told me one time that I was "born old," that even when I was little I was different from the other kids that were in the neighborhood where we used to live. That I saw things in people and could read them, and I was always looking and thinking about what was going on. Mama is right about that.

But it doesn't take an old person to know that some boys just aren't dating material. That's why I like Luke so much. I feel he has all this potential to be someone special in life and do the right thing. Doing the right thing toward other people is really, really important to me. When I was six or seven, Poppa had this job working construction, and his boss was making him work overtime but wasn't paying him extra for it like he should have. Poppa would complain to Mama about it at night, but he was afraid to say anything to the supervisor because he might lose his job and what would happen to us then…we were barely getting by back then. That boss did not do the right thing toward my Poppa.

Luke will always do the right thing toward other people; I can see that in him. And any girl he would ever date would be treated with respect and he would be sweet and kind to her and see about her needs first. I don't see those qualities in Marcus…at least not right now…maybe he will grow into them.

Camila and Hannah talk and talk and talk and I listen and nod a lot and finally Camila says she is going to say yes to going out with Marcus. Hannah says super and gives Camilla a big hug. I force a smile and say that sounds wonderful but I feel like a hypocrite for not being open and honest with her. But what was I supposed to say…I don't know. I'm really glad I'm now spending the whole lunch period Tuesdays, Thursdays, and Fridays with Luke. I eat my sandwich really quick on the way there, stop for a drink of water at a fountain, and I'm good to go. Tuesdays and Thursdays are nice with Luke, especially after we make it through the math tutoring so we can read and talk a little. But Friday lunches with Luke and our book are the highlight of my week.

Oh, I give Camila and Marcus one month of being together, maybe two…tops.

Chapter Twenty-Five: Luke

Granddaddy and I went deer hunting this past Saturday in the neighborhood. I might as well get this out of the way now. I blew a shot at a doe that was only about 12 yards away. All night I was so excited that I couldn't sleep. I kept tossing and turning and thinking about how I was going to handle things when a deer came by, and how I was going to keep calm and make a good shot and the deer wouldn't go very far and die quickly. I didn't want it to suffer when I shot it. Finally, I just gave up getting any sleep and got up an hour before I was supposed to and ate a huge bowl of oatmeal for breakfast with bananas, cranberries, and blueberries. I didn't want to get hungry when I was sitting in the blind. Dad and Mom had gone away to a race for the weekend, so I didn't have to worry about waking them up.

Granddaddy picked me up early; I think he was excited about my being excited about going. We got to the blind about an hour before sunrise, and when it's dark like that, it's just my favorite time of the day. Even in the neighborhood, I heard two screech owls whistling that creepy night song of theirs, and then as it got closer to dawn, the cardinals, and robins and Carolina wrens started singing. I just love listening to the birds. Then dawn came, and I could see better and better as every second went by.

We had been sitting there looking out the blind's front window for about 20 minutes, and this young doe came out of the woodlot and started feeding toward us. She was about 20 yards away, which is within range but her head was pointed straight on toward the blind. I needed her to turn broadside and begin feeding before I could shoot…that's what the magazines say to do. I raised my left knee, propped up my crossbow with my left elbow on my knee, and clicked off the safety so the doe wouldn't hear it when she got super close.

So she kept walking and walking and getting closer and closer and still I couldn't shoot because she was still head on toward us. My heart was just pounding and pounding and I started breathing hard and Granddaddy whispered relax, you can do this. I felt like I was going to hyperventilate. The next thing I know the deer was just, like, eight yards away right outside the window, and I raised up the crossbow just a little, and the doe, she stared daggers at the window. And I rushed the shot and I thought the arrow went right over her back and into the woods. The doe ran off and Granddaddy said did you hit her, and I said that I wasn't sure but I thought I missed. And he said that I had better go outside the blind and make sure that I missed, because it would be wrong if I did hit her and she was out there in the woods suffering.

So I climbed out of the blind and went into the woods and scared about five or six deer that were just inside the tree line and they went running and snorting through the woods and I heard other deer that I couldn't even see running and snorting, and it was just a big mess. Then I found the arrow and there was absolutely no blood on it…that confirmed what I had thought had happened, that I had blown the shot.

I went back to the blind and told Granddaddy what had happened, and he said that was okay, that I would kill the next one that came by. That made me feel a little better, but we sat there for like hours and no more deer came by. I had ruined hunting for the whole morning, I was so angry at myself. When we left, I stopped by the man's house and told him what had happened and he said that was okay, everybody messes up some time or another. Then I just blurted out and asked if we could come back Tuesday after school, and the man said yes…he was tired of the deer eating everything in his garden and stripping his fruit trees.

So I practiced and practiced with my shooting form the rest of the day Saturday and Sunday, and I worked on my breathing and being relaxed, and Granddaddy picked me up after school on Tuesday and we drove straight to the man's house. We lucked out that no deer were in his backyard right then, and we eased into the blind as quickly and quietly as we could without any deer seeing us.

About an hour later, I finally saw the first deer of the evening. She popped out of the woods 15 yards away, turned broadside and put her head down into some clover and began feeding. It happened so quickly I didn't have time to get nervous. I raised my crossbow, sucked in some air and let it out and said to myself relax, relax, relax, and shot the arrow. It went right through her chest and she sort of staggered into the woods and a few seconds later I heard this big crash. She had to be down, I just knew it.

I burst out of the blind, entered the woods, and there she was just 25 yards away—dead on the ground, she hadn't suffered one bit. I let out this yell and Granddaddy came out of the blind and by then I was standing over the deer and getting out my Buck gutting knife. I got out this sheet of paper on how to field dress a deer that I had printed from the Internet, and I went to work, saving the heart and the liver and removing the insides. Dad loves liver and onions, and I thought maybe he would be proud of me for once for bringing him something and not messing up like I do all the time with vacuuming and washing his cars.

My hands were all covered with blood, and I made this mental note that I should ask Mom for some of her dishwashing gloves to take next time I went hunting. I got blood all over my camo, and Granddaddy said there was this big streak of blood across my forehead where I must have wiped the sweat away. I didn't care about that at all. I had just killed my first ever deer!

Chapter Twenty-Six: Elly

We've been reading *Call of the Wild* in Honors English class, and just about all the boys are really into it because it's like a boy's adventure story where a dog gets kidnapped and gets sent to Alaska to become a sled dog and more and more starts acting like a husky and at times even a wolf. The book is very graphic about the way the dogs act and fight and kill, but I have to admit that the story is well written. It's still more of a guy book than one I would pick to read for myself.

When we were about halfway through the book, Ms. Hawk gave us an assignment to write a 500-word story about something that we do or have done out in nature. The guys were all asking whether they could write about the time they went fishing or camping or hunting, and a few of the girls asked if they could write about going hiking or to a summer camp, and Ms. Hawk said all those were good suggestions for papers. And I panicked because I couldn't think of anything that I had done outside and finally I asked Ms. Hawk if I could write about helping my dad with his tomato plants and she said yes. I probably wouldn't have such chubby legs if I went outside more, but I don't like to exercise and do nature stuff. She said we had a week to write the story, that it should be grammatically perfect, and she was going to project them on the Smart Board so that everyone could read what we wrote. She also said that we would peer edit each other's papers in our Bonus Points groups so that nobody would have any embarrassing mistakes. That we also had three days to write the paper and edit the paper in our groups the final two days.

So on the fourth day, I got together with Luke, Mia, and Jayla, and we started editing each other's papers. I read Luke's first; it was all about how he had killed his first deer the other day and it was just poetic, the story was so beautiful and it made me feel like I was there, and I don't know anything about hunting. Luke wrote about the birds and the night and morning and seeing the deer and then missing the shot and being determined that the next time he went hunting, he would kill one for the meat to feed his family. He wrote about how he loved his grandfather and how they were very close and the bond they had, which had been strengthened by going hunting together. I couldn't find a single grammar error in the whole paper; it was just perfect in every way.

And I told all that to Luke, and he got this embarrassed look on his face, and he said what I had said meant a whole lot to him, and he thanked me over and over. Then I said that I had to ask, how on earth does he have a B average in English when he can write like that. And Luke replied that a B was the highest he ever made in English, and the reason he didn't have an A (as Ms. Hawk had told him) was that he had not done a single grammar homework worksheet all year. I asked why not, and he said that he had to wash and vacuum cars every day after school, that even with Mia helping him, he still had to do math homework many nights that took forever, then there was history and science homework, and he didn't see any point on doing a grammar worksheet about commas that some poor fool had written and made all kinds of errors that he would never make in sentences. Why, he said, should he correct that fool's comma errors when he already knew how to use commas. It was sort of weird reasoning, but on the other hand it really wasn't. Besides at the end of a long day, Luke said all he wanted to do was read one of the books from his and Mia's book club for 15 minutes before he fell asleep.

Then I read Mia's paper and it was beautiful too. She wrote about helping her mom raise these beautiful flowers from seeds that her grandmother had brought from Mexico. That the garden was part of her heritage, and she and her mom were trying to honor that heritage but at the same time be good American citizens and learn new ways. Jayla's was next, and she wrote about the time her family traveled to South America and worked on helping poor rural families have better lives. I have to tell you I was embarrassed when my group members got to me and I had written about helping my dad a little in his tomato patch, but everybody said my paper was great. But I think they were just being polite.

You know that old saying about some people are like onions, that there are all kinds of layers to their personalities and who and what they are. I am starting to feel that way about Luke, that there is more to him than I ever realized.

Chapter Twenty-Seven: Marcus

Of course Camila said yes to me on Wednesday when I checked back in for our possible date on Friday night. I told her that Joshua and Jordan and us were going out to a really nice restaurant, and we would pick her up around 6:30. I asked Camila what her curfew was, and she said her parents said she had to be home by 10:00. I said my curfew was midnight but that Joshua and me could work with her early hours. I could tell she was impressed with what I call my 3 *S's*: smooth, sexy, and suave.

So we rolled up to her house at 6:30 sharp, and I know she had to be impressed with the wheels that were going to be her carriage for the evening. Her dad sort of had a constipated smile when he met me at the door, and I told him he had a really pretty daughter, which didn't seem to improve his disposition any. Man, when Camila came to the door, she looked freaking hot, but I know not to say something like that in front of her daddy. The inside of her house sure wasn't much to look at, but neither was the outside.

When we got to the restaurant, I ordered Surf and Turf for my entrée, and I asked her if I could order that for her. Most girls want a guy that takes charge of everything…I'm good at doing that. But Camila hesitated to say anything when I offered to order, then she finally said she didn't think she could eat that much and could she have just a little more time. Right about that time, I looked over at Joshua and Jordan and they were both staring at me and looking angry. Then Joshua gave a tight shake of his head like he was saying no and then like mouthed some words. I think what he mouthed was "grow up," which made me really mad. I know what I'm doing, and I don't need his help except to get me somewhere in his car. And that will change next year when I get my own car.

Camila finally said that she wanted flounder and a baked potato with her salad, and I said I could make that happen. After we finished the main course, Jordan asked Camila if she wanted to go to the restroom, so they took off. As soon as they left, Joshua lit into me, that I'm embarrassing him, and for me to "grow up." He's always saying that and I'm sick of it. I told him that I knew what I was doing and that I was good with the ladies. And he snapped right back and said was that why Kylee dumped me?

I told him that I dumped her, which wasn't true, but I'm sick and tired of his big brother routine and him telling me how to run my life. He said that Camila seemed like a really smart girl, that she could think for herself and didn't need my help with ordering anything, whether it was the entrée or dessert. Then he started harping on my attitude on the football team, and that he hoped to goodness that I wouldn't act like a jerk on the basketball team. That the guys had a chance to be pretty good this year, and that I should find my role and do whatever I could to make the team better, whether it was at the starting shooting guard spot or coming off the bench as the sixth or seventh man.

I told him that I would be starting as soon as I rounded into basketball shape and caught up with the other guys. And he interrupted me and said no, that I would be starting when I proved to Coach Henson that I was the best player for the spot. And that was not going to happen unless I started sharing the ball more and passing to the open shooter. I snapped right back and told him that I was the shooting guard and not the point guard, didn't he know that much and the difference between the two. He said you're a guard, stupid, shoot when you're open and pass when you're not or when someone else is open.

By now, we were really going at each other, and then all of a sudden he said shut-up, the girls were coming back, and he put on this fake smile when the girls got back, like everything was okay between us. When I get my car next year, there won't be any more double dating with you, big brother.

The waitress came back with the dessert list, and Joshua asked Jordan what she wanted for dessert, and she said key lime pie, and he said that sounded good and he would have some, too. I said the chocolate cake dish looked good to me, but Camila said to the waitress that all she wanted was a small dish of vanilla ice cream. That was good, I don't like fat chicks.

Then we drove around for a while, and Jacob drove over to Camila's house to drop her off, and I escorted her to the door and gave her a big kiss. I don't think she was expecting that; I think she was worried that her dad might have seen it. Camila has got all the makings of making a fine girlfriend.

Chapter Twenty-Eight: Mia

I was already in bed and almost asleep when the phone rang last Friday night, and I had to run to answer it before it woke up Mama and Poppa. It was Camila, and she wanted to talk about her date with Marcus, and I said I was exhausted and could we talk tomorrow morning. She asked if she could come over after breakfast and I said no, that Poppa had to work a half-day on Saturday to get extra money, and Saturday morning, Mama and I were going to mow the yard (she's going to do the front yard while I mow the back) to surprise him so he wouldn't have to do it himself when he was all tired from his job.

So Camila said how about her and Hannah coming over after lunch, and the three of us could go over the date with Marcus and analyze what happened. The tone in Camila's voice sort of hinted to me that it hadn't been the best date in the world, but what did she expect when she went out with Marcus…who is just so immature and at the same time so incredibly cocky and spoiled.

Mama and I really worked hard outside Saturday morning while my sisters cleaned the kitchen and washed the clothes. I really admire Mama for how she likes to take some of the workload off Poppa—that's how a woman should treat a man…help him and be partners with him and discuss things and make decisions together. That's how I want my relationship with the guy I marry to be, just like Mama and Poppa and the way they work together. After Mama and I finished mowing, we clipped around the house and weeded the flower garden, and we were both smiling and nodding our heads at each other. Mama and I make a good team, too.

When Poppa came home at lunchtime, he was so surprised to see the yard looking so good and the same for all of the outside and he bragged on Mama and me and made us both feel so good. Then he bragged on the work that Isabella and Emma had done inside and they were just beaming, and then he gave us all a kiss and a hug. I love my poppa! He said he was going to take all his girls out for ice cream after supper tonight.

After lunch, Camila and Hannah came over and we went for our walk. The first thing I said was how did it go, and Camila said okay she guessed, that it was her first ever date, it was hard to know if a date was supposed to be fun or not, and right then and there, I knew the date hadn't gone so well. Then Hannah said what was the problem, and Camila replied, what were the *problems*, you mean. Then I knew there had been some serious issues.

Camila said that Marcus had been bossy when they were ordering their food and all he had wanted to do was talk about himself and his football and basketball skills. She said that she got the impression that Marcus' brother Joshua was perturbed with him, too, for the way he acted, because he kept giving off this aggravated body language-type movements.

The worst thing, continued Camila, was that when they got to her house, Marcus walked to her door and then gave her this big sloppy kiss that was too hard and wet and long. And she thought her dad had come to the window when the car drove up and that maybe he had seen the kiss and would be angry with her.

The main question that Hannah had for Camila was if she was going to go out for a second date, and Camila said she thought she had to. That she had to argue and plead with her parents to go out on a date this year anyway with any guy, not just Marcus, and by not going out again, she would be like saying that her parents were right all along about not going out. I understood what she was saying and I told her so, but I thought that I had better keep my mouth shut about telling her that Marcus was my idea of a perfect loser. I got the distinct impression that Camila liked the idea of going out and having a boyfriend more than she liked staying at home and doing schoolwork…and not having a boyfriend.

While all this was going on, I remembered that Camila and Hannah had teased me about spending so much time with Luke and calling him my fixer upper project. If Luke and I had been out on a date, he would never have been bossy to me and he would have wanted to hear about how I felt about things. We talk about life and current events all the time, and Luke always wants to know about how I think about things. But Marcus is like one of those guys that has to be in control all the time. I am beginning to think that Marcus is also a fixer upper that can't ever be fixed. But that's not my problem, and before too long, I bet it won't be Camila's either.

Chapter Twenty-Nine: Luke

I hadn't had any more problems with Mrs. Burkhead in science class since the field trip, but the crap hit the fan Wednesday two days before Christmas break. She said that when we came back from the break we would start studying fish, and along with that, invasive aquatic species that don't belong in our ecosystems. I admit that I haven't been paying much attention to her since she kicked me out of class the second time. I haven't raised my hand and she hasn't called on me since. But when she started talking about fish, I really tuned in.

Mrs. Burkhead said that, for example, around here the native fishes were such ones as smallmouth bass, redbreast sunfish, and channel catfish and that the carp was an invasive species. I raised my hand at that because smallmouths were stocked around here in the 1800s. I know all about that. She kept rambling on and on, and my hand was still up and she kept ignoring me, and then she said something else that wasn't true—that smallmouths fed mostly on aquatic insects. Finally she said what is it, Luke, this had better be good.

And I told her that smallmouths were not native—that they had been stocked but had since become the most popular gamefish around here. And that smallmouths only mostly eat aquatic insects when they are small, then they turn to crawfish, minnows, and hellgrammites because it is more energy efficient for them to go after bigger prey. She got all mad and said not to contradict her, but then I said what she was saying was incorrect.

Well, she was just steaming with anger then, and the next thing I knew she called me up to her desk, was filling out one of those blame discipline referral forms and circling the usual defiance of authority-type comments, and I was on my way to Mr. Caldwell's office.

He was not happy to see me and got really mad when he started reading the discipline form. I was expecting in-school suspension...that would have been okay if I could have least explained to Mr. Caldwell what Mrs. Burkhead's mistakes were. Instead, he said there was a general science class first period, and he was going to put me in that and then switch me to general English fourth period to get me out of Mrs. Burkhead's class second semester.

I begged him to please not do that. That Mrs. Hawk was the first English teacher I had ever liked and I was making a B in there, and all I wanted him to do was Google up "smallmouth bass introduction" and "adult smallmouth foods" and he would see that I was right. I have to confess that I started to cry; it was humiliating to be 14 going on 15, sitting in the assistant principal's office and bawling like a baby, but I've hated school so much and finally there is one class that I like and I'm doing well in it except for not doing that stupid grammar worksheet homework stuff, and I'm going to be kicked out—that's not fair. I told Mr. Caldwell while I was crying that it wasn't fair.

So he looked at me crying, then turned to his computer and started to google and about two minutes later, he told me that I was right about smallmouths not being native and what they ate. He then sort of shook his head and said he was going to let me sit outside his office the rest of the period, and next period was Mrs. Burkhead's planning period, and the three of us would talk then. Then I think he sent Mrs. Burkhead an e-mail telling her to report to the office.

Well, when she got there the next period, she started in on me right away about my being rude and disrespectful and brought up the smallmouth bass incident. I hadn't said a word yet to defend myself and then Mr. Caldwell said that I needed to apologize to Mrs. Burkhead for interrupting her class, that although I had raised my hand, she hadn't called on me, and I should have waited. I apologized, even though she had—finally—called on me when I had my hand up. She had been ignoring me. But then he asked Mrs. Burkhead if she knew I was right about smallmouths not being native to our area, and also that I was right about the foods they ate at different stages of their lives. She got all red in the face and started to get mad and then she stuttered and mumbled something.

At first, I felt good about Mr. Caldwell correcting her, but then I realized that Mrs. Burkhead was going to have it in for me worse than ever now. I think he sort of wanted to make a compromise between Mrs. Burkhead and me, so he said I was going to get one period of in-school suspension during science class the next day. He said I should be mindful of being polite and respectful at all times in class and he encouraged Mrs. Burkhead to call on me more—and other students for that matter as well—when we might have an area of expertise to share with the class. He said doing so would make for good class discussions.

Mrs. Burkhead said he had an excellent point and she would "endeavor" to do just that, but there was just this little hint of sarcasm in her voice, and I don't think that old woman—she must be close to 40—is ever going to change her attitude and the way she teaches. I'll be lucky if I get a D- in her class the second semester and get a credit for the year. But at least I still get to be in Ms. Hawk's class next semester. I hate know-it-all teachers, the kind that think they never make mistakes. Then when they do, they have to cover them up.

Chapter Thirty: Elly

The last week or two during lunch, Paul, the junior center on the football team—he lives down the street from me in my neighborhood—has been dropping by my lunch table where Mary, Paige, and I eat. He has been talking mostly to me. A couple of weeks ago, Mary started dating another junior, Ian, an offensive lineman on the football team, and most of the time Ian has been with Paul when he's come by. I mean these are really big, muscular guys. Of course, Paige is still dating Allen, and where and when they go out is dependent on which one of their parents can drop them off somewhere and pick them up…so Paige is sort of the "disinterested bystander" in the little game that is being played out, and she has been quick to analyze Paul's intentions.

She says that Paul is flirting with me and testing the waters, so to speak, about whether to ask me out. Of course, my parents aren't allowing me to date this year, so I know I can't go out with him on a date-date. Paul seems to be nice enough, and I hear that his grades are pretty good, and he is very big and muscular—didn't I just say that? But he's not super good looking, if you know what I mean. He's also a little fat around his middle, but I think football linemen are sort of required to have big bellies, at least it seems that way to me—Ian's got the same build and belly, and Mary doesn't have any problems with that. And I've got a little problem with rolls around my middle, too, so I guess I shouldn't talk too much about the stomach sizes of Paul and Ian.

Well, anyway, on Wednesday Paul and Ian came by and said they were going Christmas shopping that night and would Mary and I like to come, maybe we could stop somewhere and have some coffee or ice cream or something before we went home. That since it was a school night and we were freshmen and all that, we wouldn't stay out late; we would be home before 8:30 in case we had homework or something to do.

My mind just went haywire when those two guys started talking. I mean they're both practically men and one of them is interested in me, and Paul's not particularly cute but he's not bad looking either, and the boys haven't exactly been lining up to flirt with me this year. And then I started thinking about what my parents would think and whether or not I should tell them the truth or just say something at dinner like, "Mom, Dad, some of my friends are going out Christmas shopping tonight, and they're picking me up at 6:00 to go, too, and I'll be home by 8:30 and I don't have much homework anyway tonight, so I'll be leaving in a few minutes," like it was the most casual thing in the world and just play the whole thing off like it was nothing and act like I wasn't asking them for permission, just telling them I was "going to the mall" for a little while. Which was true and all, but I was going to be driven there by a guy who is 17 and he is going to be sitting in the front seat with his girlfriend, and another guy who is 17 is going to be sitting in the backseat with me.

So I'm at the dinner table with my parents and go into my little rehearsed speech and Dad mumbles something and Mom gives me an indifferent nod of her head meaning yes, and then I really, really begin to feel guilty because deep down, I'm deceiving them, but not really because it's not a date-date thing. So a little before 6:00, they drive up and I rush out the door and down the steps like I'm going to get into a car with a bunch of girls and off we go to the mall.

As soon as we get there, we pair off immediately which I sort of expected would be the case and Ian and Mary take off somewhere and Paul and I are left to walk around and visit the stores. The first thing I think of is that I've got to buy something for Dad so that I can show it to Mom who then will know that I really was at the mall. So I go buy Dad a tie, he must have a zillion of them, so what is one more, and get it gift wrapped.

So that's out of the way, and then Paul and I start walking around and visiting stores and video game places, and he talks and talks about the football season and how upset he was about the way it ended and how he's lifting weights now and trying to bulk up some more (my gosh, how big does he want to be, he said he weighs 250). And I've got to admit that I was so bored with everything he talked about and everything we did. I don't have any interest in those macho video games that lots of guys play with them killing terrorists and zombies and the occasional vampire. It's just so immature and pointless. We must have wasted 30 minutes watching him play some game.

Paul texts Ian for us to meet up at an ice cream shop, and we go there and both guys have these huge chocolate milkshakes, and May and I just order single scoop cones. And the guys talk football some more and ask us what we thought about such and such a game and then it's 8:00 and time to head for home. So my non-date night out was pretty boring, but my dad got a gift wrapped tie out of it. And I really, really hope that none of Mom and Dad's friends saw me.

Chapter Thirty-One: Marcus

Finally, things are starting to go my way again. Tuesday night, we had a big game against Riverview, and I started out riding the pines like I usually do. We were down by eight at home with three minutes left in the first quarter when Coach Henson finally sent me in. Quentin, our point guard, called for a clear out for me so that I could isolate one-on-one against their shooting guard, and I took him to the hoop big time—two points! Talk about Mr. Microwave Offense, it took me all of five seconds to score once I hit the hardwood.

The next time down, Quentin feeds me again, and I started bulling my way to the basket, then stop on a dime, break the other shooting guard's ankles with a crossover, soar into the air and sink a silky smooth 12 footer. I'm feeling it already and yell over to Quintin to get me the ball the next time down, which he is smart enough to do. He feeds me just below the three-point line, I step back above it, then drill a three-pointer. The crowd just goes nuts, and I look into the stands real quick to see if Camila is there.

There's like 12 seconds left in the quarter when their point guard crosses midcourt when Coach Henson gives Quentin and me the signal to jump and switch. Their point gets all flustered, which, man, you can understand because the on-ball pressure is just unbelievable, and he should have called time but doesn't. The next thing that happens is that I strip him, push the ball ahead and go in for a thundering, bring-the-rim down, posterizing slam dunk right before the quarter buzzer sounds. Man, I scored nine points in three minutes, and instead of being down, we're up one.

Coach Henson has enough sense to stay with his hot hand—me—when the second quarter begins. Right off the bat, Riverview doubles me the first time I get the ball, but I feed Quentin a behind-the-back pass, and he jacks up a three—nothing but net thanks to a pretty assist from me. The very next time down, I mean the very next time down, Quentin picks the pocket of their point guard, we get out on a 2-on-1 fast break, and I slam another one home. That's 14 straight points for the old home team. We've gone from eight down to six up, and we never look back the rest of the night.

I play the whole second quarter, take the court with the starters at the beginning of the second half, and only go out for a two-minute blow at the end of the third quarter. I end up scoring 28 points, the most anybody on our team has scored this year and my personal best ever. You know, I had never really thought about playing both pro football and basketball before Tuesday night. It would be incredibly difficult, especially if my football team went to the Super Bowl. But I could play football until the Super Bowl was over, then join my NBA team for the stretch run and playoffs. It's possible, but I have to admit that it would be a long shot. I'm probably better off just to concentrate on the NFL.

Things have been going really well with Camilla, too. I can tell that she's impressed with the way I do things and take the lead and everything when we go out. She hardly says anything; she's already figured out that it's best to leave everything up to me. Most girls, deep down I really believe, want the man to be almost totally in charge. I texted her Tuesday night after my big time performance, but she didn't respond. I guess she'd already gone to bed for the night. I told her all about it the next morning in first period English when we were waiting for Ms. Hawk to start.

I've been thinking about what to get Camila for Christmas; our one month anniversary of dating will be on Friday, the last day before the break. I asked Joshua what I should get her, and he said, man, you two have only been dating for, like, four weeks, it's not time to be spending Mom and Dad's money on something like a Christmas gift for a girl you're just starting to get to know. What does he know, his advice hasn't been so great so far about anything. I swear.

Finally, I decide to buy her a sweater, which is the nice safe choice, I figure. I found one that would really look great on her, and one that she could wear when she needs to snuggle up to me. Or one that would look good on her on those cold winter days when snow closes school, and we head for the mall in the afternoon for a movie or strolling through the place.

Yep, I am on a serious roll.

Chapter Thirty-Two: Mia

Camila really wanted to talk Wednesday during lunch when she and Hannah and I finally had time to catch up with what has been going on. Camila said that Marcus texted her Tuesday night to tell her about the great game he had had, and she said that she just wanted to go to bed and not spend the next 45 minutes texting back and forth about how great a basketball player he is.

Hannah said Marcus truly did play great Tuesday night, and maybe she should have given him some encouragement, but Camila said that one thing Marcus did not lack for was self-esteem—that he had more of it than a person should have for that matter. Then Camila said she dreaded, yes she said *dreaded* the thought of Marcus probably wanting to spend a lot of time together during Christmas break, and what she really wanted to do was break up with him before Christmas because she just knew that he was going to get her an expensive Christmas gift even though they had not been dating even a month yet. And her family couldn't afford a gift for him, besides they hadn't been dating long enough to be giving gifts to each other.

Then Camila said something that was a little upsetting. She said her dad really liked Marcus and that he kept telling her what a nice house Marcus had and how she could do a lot worse. Then I finally said something, asking her how her mama felt about him and Camila said the other day her mama took her aside and said that she had the strong feeling that her daughter didn't really care for this boy. And Camila told her mama that she didn't feel special or excited when she went out with Marcus, and the things that she most thought about were how bored she was and how boring Marcus was, and if dating was like this her whole life, she could just as well become a nun.

Hannah and I laughed at the thought of Camila becoming a nun, but then I got serious and told her that if she really didn't see the relationship going anywhere, then I would support her if she decided to break up with Marcus. But Hannah chimed in, and said that she should try to work things out with Marcus because he was going to be a professional athlete one day and they make great money…which is just a ridiculous reason to date somebody, even if a guy is a great athlete. I said I disagreed with Hannah, which made her a little peeved at me (I could tell by her body language) and said that Camila should follow her heart and listen to her mama.

I don't know how the whole Camila and Marcus thing is going to work out, but at least I finally had the courage to tell her that she should break up with him if that is what she though best.

Friday morning in English when we were wrapping up our work for the first semester, when Ms. Hawk gave us an overview of what we were going to be doing second semester. She said the first thing we were going to study was *Romeo and Juliet* by Shakespeare. Then she said to go to her homepage and look under Shakespeare PowerPoints and told us that our assignment over Christmas was going to be to research one of the topics she had listed. When we drew for topics, mine was Shakespearean food, Camila's was early 1600s fashion styles, and Hannah's was on the Black Death. All of the topics seemed really interesting. I can hardly wait to get started on mine.

Then Ms. Hawk went to the list of characters for the play and gave little quick character sketches for each one. And she said for us to start thinking about who would make a great Romeo and Juliet and Marcus raised his hand and said he and Camila would be "awesome" for those parts. What Marcus said really, really embarrassed Camila. I felt like she just wanted to disappear away into the wall or something, she seemed so bothered by Marcus' remarks.

During Luke's and my Friday lunch date (I've started calling it that to Luke and he just grins when I say it, which means he's okay with it), I asked him if he would like to go to the public library over the break and do research together on our Shakespeare topics (his is on the King James Bible being put together), and he said that would be great. That he could jog there from his house or ride his bike, and I said that my house was about four miles away, and I could walk or ride my bike there.

I am super, super excited that Luke wants to spend time with me over Christmas—I mean how awesome is that! Maybe that is how best to get to know a guy, talking first as friends then becoming better friends, and then seeing if there is a spark there that is worth following through on. I know I already feel something for Luke, and I really believe he is starting to feel something for me. I sure as the world know that Camila going out with Marcus when they barely knew each other isn't the way to start something lasting.

I wonder if I should ask Luke if Ms. Hawk asks for volunteers to play Romeo and Juliet after the break, would he mind if I volunteered the two of us? I wouldn't dare volunteer us if I knew he would be embarrassed by it. Maybe I'll ask him the day we are at the library—maybe not, though.

SECOND SEMESTER

Chapter Thirty-Three: Luke

I was actually glad to come back to school on Monday after Christmas break—well, I was glad to come back to first period and Ms. Hawk's class. I wasn't looking forward to math class or renewing acquaintances with old Mrs. Burkhead or health class, or a whole heck of a lot of things. Over the break, I rode my bike three times to the library to meet Mia, and I have to confess I was excited to see her every time. I had missed talking to her. The first time we met there, I got to the library about 15 minutes earlier than we had planned I was so excited. I had missed our lunchtime talks and hanging out in the library.

I was waiting outside for her to get there, and when she got off her bike, I was so excited that I walked over and patted her on the back. I had never touched a girl with, with…I don't know what the right word is…with affection? As soon as I touched her, I got nervous that she wouldn't like that, but she grinned at me and leaned in a little and squeezed my hand, and I thought about holding her hand when we walked into the building, but I didn't. A girl, a beautiful sweet girl who is so smart…she squeezed my hand and was glad to see me…me of all people! Can you believe that.

Am I starting to have feelings for her? I don't know, maybe I am. But I do know for sure that I really enjoy being with her, and she must feel the same. We had so much to talk about. In our book club, we've read *Walden*, *1984*, and *Brave New World* all the way through. Right before break, we decided to start *White Fang* because Mia thought I would like it. So we spent part of our visits talking about that book. Then we would go online and read and discuss current events for a while. Last, we would work on our PowerPoints together and practice presenting whatever part we had finished that day.

Mia has opened up this whole other world of literature to me. I still prefer reading about sports in magazines and online, but I have to admit that there are some pretty good books out there. I mean who knew. And because she has confidence in me, I have more confidence in myself to raise my hand in English and history classes especially. I'm so very, very grateful, to her about that and for her tutoring me in math. I had a high *D* average for the semester, and that's really good for me.

After we had met for the third time at the library, Mia asked if I was hungry, that she had made two chicken sandwiches, one for her and one for me. And I said I had already eaten, but I would like one of her sandwiches, and she said she never saw me eat in school, and what did I eat for lunch. I said apricot energy bars, that Mom bought them for me for a school snack but that was all I ate at school because I was secretly putting all the money Mom gave me for school lunches in my bank account. I also put in my account all the money I earned from mowing people's lawns.

Mia asked what I was saving for, and I told her that one day I wanted to have money enough to buy some land out in the country where I could fish and hunt and live. That I knew it would take years and years but if I started saving now, that at least it would be a start. I told her that I had told my granddaddy about my dream, and he said it had been his dream too and he had never done it, and we talk about that land a lot. And he encourages me to go for it.

Mia said it was an awesome dream, and it would be so romantic to live out in the country and have a place to put down roots. And she talked about her dreams of going to college and doing something meaningful with her life and helping others, and maybe one day being able to help out her parents when they were old. She is so awesome and sweet.

Then Mia asked if it would be all right if she volunteered for us to be Romeo and Juliet when second semester started in Ms. Hawk's class. At first when she said that, I got nervous at the thought of having to do all that reading in Shakespeare-style English, and I think she could tell that I was nervous, and she said with one of those smiles of hers that she was confident that we would make a good team, and I would do great. I smiled back and said okay, and she squeezed my hand again.

I tell you when she smiles at me...and those times when she has squeezed my hand...I think I can do things...that I am somebody.

Chapter Thirty-Four: Elly

I lied to my parents over Christmas break, and now I'm probably going to have to tell a few more lies to get myself out of this mess. Paul texted me the day after Christmas and asked if I would like to double date with Ian and Mary. We would go out to dinner at Olive Garden and then go see a movie at the mall. I can tell myself that the shopping trip with them to the mall was not really a date, and it really wasn't, but it obviously wasn't a shopping trip with a bunch of girls like I hinted that it was to my parents. So I really didn't lie there.

So I texted back that I wasn't allowed to date yet, but if I could convince my parents to drop me off at the mall and that one of Mary's parents was going to drop me off at home afterwards, then I thought the whole thing would work out. Paul said for me to give my plan "a shot" and would wait to hear back from me.

I'm not one of those "bad" girls that is constantly lying to her parents and teachers, but the more I think about Mary and Paige being able to date, it makes me angry that my parents are so strict and conservative. On the other hand, I've been just sick with worry and guilt that my parents could find out about my lying and how they would be disappointed in me, because Mom said she would drop me off at the mall, and it would be all right for one of Mary's parents to pick me up later.

The weird thing is that I don't really like Paul all that much. He's not bad looking and he dresses really well, but he's not much of a talker—at least about things that I'm interested in. My first real date with a guy was, there's no other way to say it, really, really boring and blah. The dinner was good, and it was nice for a guy to pay for it, but all Mary and I did was nod our heads a lot, then listen to Paul and Ian talking about this year's football season, next year's football season, and who was going to win the Super Bowl. They had a lot of arguments about that one, Paul saying the Patriots and Ian saying the Packers. I mean, really, who in their right mind cares. Finally, Paul asked me who I thought was going to win, and I don't even know the names of the teams that are in what he called the playoffs. But because he said the Patriots were going to win, I said something like oh, yes, "it looks like the Patriots to me." And those were my big, profound comments during dinner.

After we had eaten the main course, both guys wanted dessert and they insisted that Mary and I both order too. Paul ordered Chocolate Mousse Cake, so that was what I ordered, and I was really full and didn't even want any. Paul talked about having to gain 20 pounds for the next football season, and I thought if I kept on going out with him, I would weigh 220 pounds one day, and he would weight 320 and wouldn't we be the pair.

The movie was something I would never have gone to on my own or with friends. I don't even remember the name of it. It was something about two guys getting revenge for something that had been done against them; I'm not sure what it was, maybe I missed that part of the movie…my attention span was sort of clicking on and off. So the two guys went about blowing up stuff that belonged to the bad guys and then at the end of the movie, the good guys and the bad guys had this long, boring hand-to-hand fight with lots of things smashed over heads and bodies. And the good guys killed the bad guys. Yeah, right, nobody saw that coming, right? The only thing that amazed me was that the whole thing was PG-13; the reviewers must have fallen asleep during the movie like I almost did.

So after the movie was over, the boys wanted to go get milkshakes, and I felt like I had to force feed myself a single dip mint chocolate chip ice cream cone. Then on the way home, the boys wanted to talk about how great the movie was and then the conversation turned to football and we ended up at my house. The best thing that happened all night was that all the lights were out at my house, and I had been worried all night that they wouldn't be. Paul opened the car door for me then gave me this long, sloppy, rough kiss on the lips, so my first kiss from a boy really wasn't what I would call life changing. It was sort of blah like the whole evening.

Three days later, Paul texted me and asked if I would like to double date again when we got back to school, that there was another great movie coming out. I can't even remember the name of it. I lied to him and said my parents saw me leave the car and I was grounded for a month...maybe we could go out again after that. That lie just blurted out from my mouth. I didn't even plan it or anything. Now who I am going to lie to next time—Paul or my parents or both—when that month is over, and Paul asks me out again.

Chapter Thirty-Five: Marcus

My second semester is off to a fantastic start…things couldn't be going better! When I got back to school on Monday, first up was Ms. Hawk's class. She said we were ready to start *Romeo and Juliet*, and did she have any volunteers for the two main characters. I raised my hand first and said that Camila and me would play the parts, and Ms. Hawk said that would be great. I looked over at Camila after I said that, and she sort of looked away, showing how shy she is. I like for a girl to be shy and submissive around me; it shows that she knows I'm in charge and that she trusts me to make good decisions.

After class, I asked Camila if she would come to the game Tuesday night and root me on and could she wear the sweater to school on Tuesday that I got her for Christmas and again on Tuesday night. That Joshua and Jordan were going to take me home, and maybe the four of us could go somewhere after the game and get a quick bite or something. She said she didn't know if her parents would let her go out on a school night, and she said the sweater was very nice and thanked me for it again. That she would let me know in first period Tuesday about going to the game and all. I know her dad really likes me, she told me that, so I expect we're on for tomorrow night. Got to tend to the ladies, you know.

Things kept getting better and better throughout Monday. At practice that afternoon, Coach Henson put me with the starting unit while we were doing our drills, and I stayed with them the whole time. Then when practice was over for the day, he told me I would be starting at shooting guard Tuesday night and to get plenty of rest because we were going to have a tough game against Springfield. If you ask me, I should have been starting long ago, but at least give credit to Coach Henson for finally wising up. Coach Dell never used me the right way during football season, especially in the last few games.

Tuesday morning, Camila told me her parents wouldn't let her go out on a school night, but thanked me "very much" for asking her, and I said I understood but I was still disappointed. Then I asked her why she didn't have my sweater on like I had asked her, and she said that it didn't match her outfit for the day. I said to be sure to wear it tomorrow, no sweat, that it would go good with that short little blue mini-skirt of hers.

Tuesday night, there's no other way to say it, but I dominated all night long. Quentin and me were in rhythm all night long, and we were in sync from the get-go. Right off the tip, Quentin fed me for a baseline three, and I was just warming up. The next trip down the floor, I drove hard to the basket and made this beautiful up and under move that posterized, absolutely posterized, their power forward. I mean I made that dude look silly.

By halftime, I had sixteen points, Quentin had seven assists, and we were up by five, which should have been more, but Springfield's shooting guard got some lucky bounces on a couple of threes. I have to tell you that Coach Henson took me out for about four minutes halfway through the second quarter, or I would have had even more points. Coach Henson barked at me and said I wasn't focusing enough on defense and letting my man get by me too much. Man, I can't play all-star style offense and defense all the time. I'm carrying the team on offense—get real, Henson.

Anyway, when the second half started, I came out on fire. I mean I really lit up the crowd—Camila should have been there to see me. It all started when Quentin and me got out on a 2-on-1 break, and I slammed that sucker down with authority and the crowd just went wild…absolutely, freaking maniac-type wild. The next time down, I was feeling it and shot a long three, but it rimmed out, but our center Eric tapped it in, and we were up by 9, and we never looked back. I poured in three more threes, made a one-handed slam on a fast break, and ended up with 29 points and we won by 13…and it wasn't that close. In case there were any scouts in the crowd, I even worked on my passing, feeding Eric and Quentin for buckets late in the fourth quarter. I mean, what a dominating performance.

Wednesday morning in English class, Camila and me finally got to read our parts for the first time, and I could tell Ms. Hawk was impressed. I've got to tell you that that Old English writing of Shakespeare's is hard to read, and I don't know what the heck is going on in that play. But my life is going so great now, that I can put up with a little aggravation. Our next game is Friday night against Stephenson, and I'm planning to bust the 30-point barrier. I just may pour in 35; who knows, a 40-point night is possible with the way I'm playing.

Chapter Thirty-Six: Mia

On the way to school on Wednesday, Camila told me on the bus that she was going to break up with Marcus as soon as she got the chance, that she couldn't stand being "his lady" anymore. That he was absolutely smothering her with demands on what to wear and what to do and not once in the six weeks that they had been dating had he ever asked her about her thoughts or opinions on anything and it was just me, me, me with Marcus and everything that they did or talked about and he was stuck up and self-centered

When Camila got started complaining it was, like, she couldn't stop. She complained about Marcus' ego and how she was tired of hearing about how much money he was going to make playing pro football and basketball and how hard it was going to be to juggle both sports at the same time, that somebody named Bo Jackson had done it and so could he…"no sweat." She said if she heard him say "no sweat" one more time to her, she would scream. Camila went on and on, and I thought, well, she and Marcus lasted six weeks, that's not bad; I wasn't sure they would last a month, and I knew it would be over between them in two months. But I didn't need to tell Camila all that, she had figured it for herself and that was good. Hannah, who was sitting behind us, was listening the whole time, and she said maybe Camila could give Marcus one more chance, and both Camila and I glared at her at the same time, and Hannah didn't say one more thing about second chances.

Then Camila told me that she needed to find a guy like Luke, that she really liked the way the two of us operated together, and that we were a "really cute couple." I told her that Luke and I weren't a couple, that we weren't dating, that we just hung out together. And Camila said, "Oh, please, everybody can see you two are a couple, and the way you smile at each other all the time." Then she said, it was just a matter of time before Luke and I started to date, probably our sophomore year when my parents said I could date. All I said was that I liked Luke a lot, and he was very sweet and we talked all the time.

I didn't want to say anything more, but I have to tell you that I've been thinking more and more about Luke and I going out on our first date and how great it would be. And I know it won't be until next year, but I confess that I worry some too that my poppa won't like me going out with a boy who's not Hispanic. I don't know how Mama would feel about that, but I think she would take my side if Poppa was against it. I wouldn't ever want to disobey my parents, but if I explained to them how sweet and wonderful Luke is, I think they would understand…at least, I hope so.

Wednesday during lunch after we had gone through the line and gotten our food, Elly came up to us and asked if she could sit with us—that her "lunch bunch" of Paige and Mary were off sitting with their boyfriends. Of course we said sure— I really like Elly and would like to get to know her better. Paige wants to sit with Allen, and Mary sits with Ian and Paul and some of the other football players and Elly really didn't want to sit with a bunch of upperclassmen and their girlfriends. Then Hannah said she had heard that Elly had gone out with Paul over the break and asked how that had gone, and Elly groaned and said "don't ask," so we took it that she didn't particularly have a grand old time. So we went back to discussing what we had been talking about all through the lunch line, Camila's soon to come breakup with Marcus, and Hannah asked Elly what she thought, and she said now was not a very good time to ask her about dating and boys. That her first date, though she couldn't say it was "the pits," it really wasn't what you would call a "night filled with glamor."

We all laughed at that, and it was right after that that Marcus came by our lunch table, and what happened next wasn't pretty. First, Marcus, asked why Camila wasn't wearing his sweater like he had asked, and Camila said she hadn't worn it yet. Then Marcus asked if she wanted to go out to Pizza Hut with Joshua and his girlfriend after the basketball game Friday night, and all Camila said was no. Then Marcus asked why not, and she said could they go somewhere and talk in private. Then Marcus got mad and said Camila could say whatever she wanted to say in front of us.

I had never seen Camila act smart-alecky toward anyone before, she's really polite, but she said really sarcastic-like that she was glad he had finally given her permission to say something and what she wanted to tell him was that she was breaking up with him. He got this really shocked look on his face, and I thought he was going to try to talk her out of it at first, but then he said, "no sweat," there were other fish in the sea, and there were lots of other girls in this school that would love to go out with him. And he just turned and walked away.

Elly then said if there was big-time drama like this every day at our table, maybe she had better go somewhere else to sit. And we all laughed, and I told Camila I was proud of the way she handled the whole dumping the guy thing, and even Hannah said that Camila could do better in the man department. Elly said we should celebrate our new quartet and Camila being single again with chocolate ice cream cones, which seemed like a pretty good idea to all of us. There's nothing better than chocolate when you've had a tense day.

Two Weeks Later: Snow Day

Chapter Thirty-Seven: Luke

Thursday in the library, Mia and I had finished up my math tutoring and were cruising the Internet before deciding what our next book club read was going to be. All day long, everybody had been talking about the weather forecast for Friday, and since Mia and I don't have cell phones we decided to check out weather.com for ourselves. The prediction showed that there was going to be three inches of snow Friday morning, which would be good enough to close school, but not so deep that would keep the kids from going to the mall on Friday afternoon and hanging out, which was why everybody seemed so excited about the snow coming.

Mia and I studied the forecast and then I said that I didn't want to miss our book club meeting and would she mind walking to the library and us having our get-together. She said that would be awesome, that if it snowed her poppa wouldn't be able to go to his construction job, and he could babysit her sisters while she met me. We then figured out where we could meet about a mile from the library and that both of us would have to roughly walk about two or so miles to meet up. She said she could ask her mama to pick her up around 5:15 because she would have to be at work at the doctor's office no matter what. I said I didn't mind walking back home, that maybe I could even get some running in if the snow had melted off the sidewalks much. Then she squeezed my hand and told me thanks for wanting to get together like that, and I tell you when she does that and says things like that, it make me feel so good about myself like nothing else does.

So we decided to meet at the junction of Salem Avenue and Main Street around 1:00 and that would give us about four hours of being together with both the mile-walk and reading time. We had never spent so much time together before, and I was so excited I got there at 12:30. I didn't mind waiting in the cold for her, and she must have been excited, too, because she was there by 12:40.

We started off walking on the sidewalk, and it was pretty clear of snow, so we were just heading for the library and talking about all the possibilities for books to read that Mrs. Kendel and Ms. Hawk had suggested, and I was just so happy to be with her, and I could tell that she was so happy to be with me…and it was just great. Then this most amazing and wonderful thing happened. She slipped on some ice, which wasn't amazing and wonderful, but I caught her and kept her from falling, which was very good, and held her hand to sort of help her over a rough patch that was like twenty yards long, then the sidewalk cleared, but she didn't let go of my hand.

We kept walking, and I stopped talking and I got nervous about still holding her hand because the sidewalk was really clear by then. And I think Mia could tell I was a little nervous about holding her hand, and all she said was "I like it," and then she squeezed my hand, and I held hers just a little bit tighter, and we walked the rest of the way there hann-hand. I haven't had a lot of things in my life to make me happy—no the word is *euphoric*, extremely happy—except having some really good days fishing and killing that doe last fall. But nothing ever has made me as happy, as euphoric, as walking along with Mia and holding her hand. I'm not what you would call a lady's man, I mean look at me. I've grown maybe an inch this school year, so I'm like 5'8" and 140—nobody's going to cast me as the leading man in a romance movie about high school kids.

But there I was walking down Main Street with definitely the smartest girl in the ninth grade, definitely one of the prettiest, and in my opinion, she and Elly are definitely the sweetest girls in the whole class. And I'm holding her hand, it was freaking unbelievable... me with her. And she likes me for myself and cares about what I have to say and overlooks the fact that I'm as dumb as a board in math.

We got to the library, and Mia got out the reading list that Mrs. Kendel and Ms. Hawk had helped with and on it were *Grapes of Wrath*, *Things Fall Apart*, *Invisible Man*, *Black Boy*, and *As I Lay Dying*. We decided to go online and read information about what all the books were about and then write down on a scratch sheet of paper what our top two choices were and see how they matched up. It was amazing, but both of us had *Grapes of Wrath* as our first choice, and I asked her why that was hers, and she said we had studied the 1930s earlier in the year and that she wanted to learn more about that time period, and I said that was why I picked it, too.

So we each checked out a copy of *Grapes of Wrath*, and we sat together on a sofa in the back of the library, and for the next three hours, we read for a little while about the Joad family, then talked about what we had read for a little while, then sometimes talked about other things, and then the next thing we knew it was almost 5:00, and I said I had better go because I would barely have time to make it home before dark and there would be some slick patches on the sidewalk. And she said her mama would be there soon to pick her up. And we squeezed each other's hands one last time for the day, and I left. It was just about the best day of my life. No, it was the best day of my life—even better than when I killed my first deer.

Chapter Thirty-Eight: Elly

I was still asleep when Mom came in to wake me up on Friday. I looked over at the alarm clock and it said 9:00 and then I looked out the window as Mom had just opened the blinds, and I could see that snow was still falling, so I quickly realized why she had let me sleep so late. Then she said that Daddy had left for work, and my brothers were still asleep and did I have anything I wanted to tell her about anything I had been doing recently. That she had run into Paul's mother yesterday evening at the grocery store when she decided to stock up on a few things before the snow came.

I knew I was in big trouble, and Mom knew I knew, and then she said something like, "You can imagine my surprise when Paul's mother said her son really had a nice time going out with Elly the other night and hoped they could go out again real soon." So Mom asked me how was she to go about dealing with a statement like that, and did I have any recommendations for a response. Then, hurrying on and not yet giving me time to say something, Mom said that, interestingly, over Christmas, she had talked my father into letting me date second semester of my ninth grade year, that she had been impressed with my grades and maturity, and that the next time I asked if I could go out on a date, the answer was going to be yes. And then Mom asked had she "been in error" concerning her opinion on my maturity and that's when I burst into tears and buried my head into her lap and said I was so sorry.

While I was crying, she asked if I had told any more lies, and I said yes, that I had told Paul that she and Dad had seen me come in late on our date and that I was grounded for a month. She laughed at that and then said that that statement was no longer a lie and that I was now "indeed," she said, grounded for a month, and that if the snow stopped and melted a little this afternoon, I would not be allowed to go to the mall or anywhere else. Mom then told me how much she loved me, that I had always been a responsible young lady and that she didn't expect any more "trouble." and I promised her that I would never again lie to her.

Now, Mom said, that that is over, how was your date the other night? It's time for some girl talk she said. I teared up a little about that, and I told her that the date was boring, that Paul and Ian only wanted to talk about football and stuff and Mary told me later she was bored, and I had so hoped that my first date with a boy would be really special and magical and it definitely had not been, and then I confessed that Paul had kissed me when we got out of the car and the kiss was all blah like the date.

Then Mom said her first date had been with a boy named Jonathan, that he had taken her to the movies when she was in the tenth grade, that he had tried to kiss her three times in the movie and finally she let him and all she remembered about the kiss was that that boy should have been "introduced" to some mouthwash before he was allowed outside the house, and maybe been "tutored" on how to use the right amount of cologne as well. She said she went out with him two weeks later for their second date, and the mouthwash, cologne, and kissing were all still issues, and she decided that he was not worth a third date, that she didn't want to waste her time "bringing him up to speed" on dating.

I laughed at all that and then I asked her about her first date with Daddy, and she said she liked him from the start, but she didn't want him to know that at first because she was afraid he would get "too cocky," that they had started dating their senior year in college, and when it was time to graduate, they decided that they didn't want to let each other out of their lives and got engaged. It was the best decision she ever made, Mom said.

Then Mom asked if I minded if she gave me some more advice, and I said no, that I needed some help with this whole dating ritual thing and Mary and Paige weren't as clueless as I was, but they weren't much better. And Mom said please, please feel free to come talk to her anytime; that, if I ever got into a situation where I was nervous or scared while I was out on a date, to call Dad or her, and they would come get me, no questions asked. Third, that high school boys, generally, she said, were not as mature as girls (well, duh, I knew that) even though I had recently tried to "disprove that theory," that I should think about giving Paul another chance when my month of being grounded was over. That he seemed like a nice boy.

Finally, she asked if I was interested in any other boys, maybe ones that were my same age. And I started to tell her that I really liked Allen but he was dating Paige, and that Caleb was smart and good looking but was dating some stupid JV cheerleader, and that I liked Luke a lot, but that I thought he had something going with Mia. But then I thought I didn't want to share any of those things, and I said something like I didn't think anyone else was interested in me, which was definitely the truth.

Mom smiled and said we should go make some pancakes and later make some brownies for everybody for dinner, but that the two of us would make a secret batch just for us for the afternoon when the boys were out playing in the yard. I love my mother.

Chapter Thirty-Nine: Marcus

Joshua came into my room Friday morning and woke me up, even though it was a snow day and I had a game that night if the weather cleared, and I needed my rest. Like he has a habit of doing, he started in on me while I was still rubbing the sleep out of my eyes. He said he had good news and bad news and which did I want first, and I said the good.

To my surprise, the good news was that he had been very impressed with my shooting guard play, that I was shooting very well and was showing "excellent quickness." He also said that I had waited patiently for the chance to start and hadn't given Coach Henson any "unsolicited, unwanted coaching advice" or in other words "lip" like I had Coach Dell. My brother told me that his only criticism of my play was that I was still looking to shoot first instead of passing first, that if I tried to be a more multi-dimensional player, that whoever was guarding me would have to play the pass, the shot, and the drive which would open it up more for me to shoot. I told him I had never thought of it that way, but he was right. If whoever is guarding me doesn't know what I'm going to do, that will only result in more shot opportunities for me. Finally, he gave me a huge compliment and made me think of something that I had never thought of. He said that I just might be a better basketball player than football player, and that I ought to keep that possibility in mind down the road, that maybe the sport I should concentrate on for the long run might be basketball.

Then I told Joshua that I really appreciated the compliments, so what was the bad news?

The bad news, he said, was that too much of the time I was an" insufferable little jerk," that he was sick of it, and that even Jordan had commented on how immature I was, and Mom and Dad were worried about it too because he had overheard them talking, and Jordan didn't want to double date any more with me and whoever I was going with at the time unless some serious changes were made in my attitude. He laid so much on me at first, that I didn't have time to take it all in, especially the part about me being insufferable. I confess that I had to look it up on my phone later and the definition was "unbearable to be with," which was a little harsh if you ask me, and not true at all. But that part about Jordan not wanting to double date with me was more than a little scary because I can't drive this year and most of my sophomore year and how I am going to go out with the ladies if I don't have a car.

Then Joshua said he had one more bad thing to discuss. He said I had already gone through two girlfriends and the year was barely half over and at the rate I was being dumped by women, I would run out of girls to date by my junior year. He said if I would promise to at least act in a mature fashion, he would see to it that I have a blind date next Friday night with Jordan's first cousin Tameka who goes to Westside High School. Joshua said she's a freshman like I am and very pretty and very sweet,according to Jordan. But if I should greet her like I'm the planet's gift to women, then Jordan would see to it that it was both my first and last date with her, and the era of our double dating days would be over.

So I said no sweat, I can behave and be mature, and my brother said, that was fine, but I had one more thing to promise. I asked him what was that, and Joshua said that I was to promise three things, based on what he and Jordan had talked about. First, I was going to ask what were Tameka's opinions about various things, and I was not to talk about things just from my perspective until she had finished and gotten her comments in.

Second, I was not to use the terms, "my lady," "my woman," or any two dozen or other similar combinations of words when I was talking to Tameka. That nobody was going to be my lady unless I grew up some more, and that using all these ridiculous phrases about girls was another thing that was insufferable about me. And the third was that I was in no position to tell anyone else how to act or think, and life would go a lot smoother for me once I learned that. So I thanked Joshua for looking after my best interests. After all what else could I do, tell him off and have to wait until the second semester of my sophomore year when I would have a car and have a chance to go out.

You know, maybe I should turn down the heat two or three clicks with the ladies. Joshua has been going with Jordan for almost two years, and things seem to be going really well between them. He must know something about women. But I don't want to admit to him that he may know more about women than I do.

Chapter Forty: Mia

I had the most wonderful snow day with Luke on Friday when school was cancelled. We agreed to meet in the afternoon after the roads had been cleared and the snow had mostly melted off the sidewalks and walk about a mile to the library so that we could have our weekly Friday book club meeting. I have been wanting to spend more time with him and maybe even hold hands with Luke, because I've been having feelings for him and I want to get to know him better and maybe date him my sophomore year when Mama and Poppa have said I could start dating.

Well, when we walking along, I lost my balance and Luke kept me from falling and held my hand just to steady me. It felt so good to hold his hand, and I didn't want him to let go, so I held his hand extra tight and squeezed it, and he smiled and it was just the most awesome feeling. When we got to the library, we picked out *Grapes of Wrath* for our next book and we spent hours that just flew by talking and reading about the book and just everything from school to what jobs we would like to have in high school and in life and just everything. He's a good listener and he cares about what I think about and what I have to say.

After Luke left, Mama came by to pick me up about 20 minutes later because I had called her that morning to say that I was going to walk to the library and would she pick me up on her way home from work. I was so happy about my day with

Luke that I wanted to tell her about him and how wonderful he was, so I did. I started off by telling her that there was a guy at school in most of my classes that I liked a lot, and I just wanted her to know that because I thought she would want to know and I didn't want to keep things from her.

Mama smiled when I said that, and she said was the boy Henrique from down our street, that she was good friends with his mother, and Poppa liked his family, too. And I said no that he was a nice boy, but I wasn't interested in him. So she wanted to know who the boy was, and I said it was Luke who lives on the other side of town, and we spend three lunch periods a week together in the library; and on Fridays, we have a book club where we're the only members and we pick out books to read, and that Luke was in my honors English, history, and science classes together and that he has a lot of ability. I didn't want to get into Luke's grades in math and science, because Mama wouldn't like that he was making a *D* in both of them.

Mama sort of frowned a little when I said the word *Luke*, and she asked if he were a Hispanic boy, and I said no, and then she said that Poppa might not like me being close friends with a guy that wasn't Hispanic. Her saying that got me a little scared, and I said that Luke is the sweetest boy in my classes, and he always treats me with respect and cares about what I have to say and how I think about things. I told her that I knew I was too young to date this year, and I would never date Luke or anybody else behind Poppa's and her back. But next year when they had said I could go out on dates, I would be really excited if Luke asked me out, and I would say yes if he did.

Mama frowned again and went a little while without saying anything, then she said that she wasn't going to tell Poppa about this, that it would be just between us for now. Then Mama asked what Luke's father did for a living, and I told her that he worked at the plant and ran a used car lot from their house. And Mama said now she knew who Luke's family was, and she had heard a rumor that his daddy had been in trouble with the police. I told her that Luke had told me about that one time, that he was embarrassed about what his father had done with the stolen cars and getting parts from them and selling them, and that he was never going to be like his father when he grew up.

Mama still didn't seem to be happy about the whole Luke thing, but she didn't seem angry, either, and I was really trying to read her and figure out what she was thinking about my being friends with him. Finally, I asked her if she would be prejudiced against him because he was white, and she said definitely not, she was more concerned that he came from a rough family. And I told her that hadn't she and Poppa always said that we shouldn't be judged in a bad way because my grandparents came here illegally, and she said, yes that was true but our situation was different. And I said I didn't see how, that I just wanted to be close friends with a really nice boy, and I wanted her to be happy and okay with me having such a good friend.

I didn't say I was sorry that I had told her about Luke and me spending the afternoon together, but I did think that maybe I should have kept the whole thing to myself because now she might be suspicious every time I leave the house, and I don't want my parents to ever feel that they can't trust me.

So finally I said that there was one more thing that I wanted to tell her, and she said what, and I said that Ms. Hawk had asked me to be on her Yearbook staff next year as the feature's editor, that being on the staff would look really good on my college applications. And Mama said she was very happy for me, and I told her that I was one of only three people in my English 9 Honors class that Ms. Hawk had asked to be on the staff. Mama asked who were the others, and I told her that Elly and Luke were the other two students and that Elly was going to be a photographer and Luke was going to be the sports editor. I have to confess that I told her about the Yearbook news because I wanted to let her know that Ms. Hawk had a high opinion of Luke. That Luke was going to be on the Yearbook staff was definitely in his favor Mama said, so I then knew that she knew that Luke has something going for him. I didn't think Mama would act this way when I told her about Luke, but I think I've smoothed things over at least a little.

Dating
on the Mind

Chapter Forty-One: Luke

I've been thinking a lot about Mia ever since we went to the library on that snow day three weeks ago. Of course, we still spend the entire lunch period Friday in the library together for our book club meeting, but now she doesn't even bother to get a quick bite to eat in the cafeteria on Tuesdays and Thursdays, so we can have more time to talk and read after she finishes tutoring me in math. I think she must eat a banana or granola bar on the way. On Fridays, I bring an extra apricot energy bar for her to eat.

What I've been thinking a lot about is how to ask her out for a date next fall when we come back to school. I was 15 in late December, so that means I can get my learner's permit in early June right after school lets out. Mom said she would help me learn how to drive. One good thing, the only good thing, about living at a used car lot is that we will have plenty of clunkers around for me to drive. Then in late March next year, I will be able to get my driver's license.

But I don't want to wait until next March to go out with Mia. I want to ask her out when the school year starts next August. I don't want to wait until later because I'm afraid some other guy will ask her out because she's so smart and sweet and pretty. And I don't want to ask Mom to drive us somewhere because that would just be the pits, sitting in the backseat with a girl and your mother, for gosh sakes, making stupid small talk with her and driving you to the mall…that would just be humiliating and embarrassing.

I also am worried about something else about asking Mia out. Dad is always ranting about "Mexicans taking all the jobs of good Americans," and how he can't stand working with them at the plant, that they are just as bad as the blacks and the Jews that have ruined this country. Mom doesn't say anything when Dad is ranting on and on, but what worries me a lot, too, is that she doesn't disagree with him. Does she feel the same way? I asked Granddaddy about how he feels about what Dad calls the "minorities," and he told me that he didn't raise Dad to be like that, but he long ago gave up on trying to change his mind, that it just caused them to argue all the time. I'm scared of Dad's temper, I told Granddaddy, and I'm not going to argue with him. Granddaddy told me to always try to "swallow my anger" when dealing with Dad and people like him, to keep my emotions under control and appear calm, though my stomach might be churning on the inside. Granddaddy told me to judge people by their behavior and how they treat others. I trust my granddaddy. The teachers in school talk all the time about young people having a need for role models, and I'm proud that he's mine.

So all this means that I'm going to have to find some way to take Mia out somewhere. We can't just ride our bikes to the mall and do something, besides I hate the mall. I hate it when Mom takes me there to get clothes…all those people and all those stores, I just hate it. Anyway, who would want to go out with a sophomore guy on a "bike date" to the mall. How am I going to compete with some junior or senior with a car and they ask Mia out for a nice dinner somewhere. I've never even been to what Mom and Dad call "fancy restaurants." I think I would like to go to one though, to see what it would be like…to take Mia to one…to show her how much I like her. It would be really expensive, though, but she would be worth it. I've saved a lot of money from mowing lawns, and not eating lunches at school, but I want to use that money one day to buy land out in the country to live on.

Maybe Mia wouldn't mind if we rode our bikes to the national forest and we went hiking and had a picnic? Maybe she would like that. I guess that wouldn't be very romantic, but neither is tutoring me twice a week for math…she says she enjoys helping me out. Maybe she would just be glad to be with me…but it's hard to believe that any girl would be happy to be with me. No, that's not true, Mia would be, at least I hope she would…yes, I believe she really would. This whole dating thing is confusing. Girls like going on picnics, somewhere I've heard that.

Or maybe we could go ride our bikes to the river and have a picnic there and go fishing…that wouldn't be as good as riding them to the national forest, though. Maybe we could ask our parents to drop us off at the mall and meet up there and go to a movie. But Mom would probably be suspicious if I asked her to drop me off at the mall. Maybe I could ask Granddaddy …yes, that would be better than asking Mom. I wouldn't mind going to the mall to see a really good movie if I was going to be with Mia. I don't know what I'm going to do, I've got to think some more on this. But I am definitely going to ask Mia out for a date next year when school starts.

Chapter Forty-Two: Elly

Well, just like clockwork when my month of being grounded was almost over last Monday, Paul dropped by my lunch table at school where I was eating with Mia, Camila, and Hannah. Paul said he was going to get some ice cream, and he asked if I would like to come too. I took that as a hint that he wanted to talk to me in private; it was all so obvious, and the girls all gave me knowing looks when I got up to go with him.

Paul grinned at me (he's not a bad guy at all, he's just boring to be with) and said by his "calculations" that the end of my grounding would be Friday and was I available Saturday night to go out and do something. That Ian had been thinking about taking Mary bowling and out for pizza afterwards, and if I was interested, we could all double date and maybe meet at the mall and go from there, since I wasn't allowed to date yet.

But I said, and I must not have been thinking at all, that my parents had given me permission to date now, and there was no need for me to sneak around like last time. And he said awesome, that he would drive and after he picked up Ian and Mary, he would pick me up at my house around 6:00 and we'd go from there. Before I even had time to think about whether I actually wanted to go on a second date with him, he was gone, the date was already arranged. How can I be so stupid!

I wasn't sure whether or not I even wanted to go out with Paul a second time, and here everything was all arranged and I couldn't go after him, telling him, wait, there's been a misunderstanding. So I just decided to go bowling…maybe it wouldn't be so bad after all.

But then I got into a real tiz, what on earth was I going to wear. I mean, I was going to have my butt and backs of my legs visible to Paul and Ian most all of the night, and what were they going to be thinking when they saw all that…here comes Ms. Big Butt the whale up to roll another ball down the lane. How am I going to lose 20 pounds by Saturday at 6? So I immediately texted Mary about what was she going to wear. I had started to go find her, but, again I'm so stupid, she would be sitting with Ian and Paul and some of the other football players and obviously I couldn't go over there and start discussing my butt and leg problems.

Mary and I texted back and forth all during fourth period science, and finally we both decided that this was not a problem that could be solved through texts, especially when Mrs. Burkhead glared at me when she saw that I had been texting by holding my phone between my legs, instead of paying attention to her never ending boring lecture on the importance of flagellates in the ecosystem. I have an A in that class, but she's an awful teacher.

So Mary and I sat together on the bus, and we debated the pros and cons of what to wear Friday night. Mary decided that she was going to wear a skirt that came just two inches above her knees, so that when she dipped to throw the ball, Ian would see some more of her legs but not too much, and she suggested that I wear a skirt like that which was an absolute non-starter as far I was concerned. Mary said I had nice legs—bless her for saying that—but I know better and finally I decided on my usual option—loose fitting jeans with a long blouse…the safe choice.

When Saturday night came Daddy insisted that Paul had to come knock on the door to talk to him for a bit since it was my first date with Paul or any other boy, which sent me into another tiz because it was our second date and what if Paul let it slip that we had gone out before. Then I could be grounded again before I even left the house. But Daddy did almost all the talking while Paul was standing there next to me nodding his head and saying yes sir a lot, and we got out of there with no damage done.

The whole bowling thing was just a total disaster from the start. When we got there, all of those silly looking special bowling shoes were smelly and none of them fit, but I finally found a pair that I could put on. The first time I threw the ball, or is it rolled, who knows, it's a stupid sport...I threw the ball straight into the gutter. I thought I was done for that inning, no that's baseball, that round, right? But Paul said I got another chance, and he held my arm and had me practice the throwing motion and told me how to walk up to this line, but not cross it, and then "let her rip." I'm taking he meant the ball to rip, not my jeans...that would be so embarrassing if Ms. Big Butt exploded out of her jeans in front of everyone.

So I threw the ball again and this time, it went, like, 10 more feet down the aisle than last time before it fell into the gutter, I got that term right for sure...gutter ball, that's what Paul and Ian kept saying I was doing with the ball. And so it went for most of the time at the bowling place. I ended up scoring a 42 and Mary made a 53, which wasn't much better...what is a good score, a 100? Who cares. I don't remember what the guys scored, I really didn't care.

Afterwards, we went out for pizza, and they ordered three with all the toppings. Both of them ate a whole pizza each... they went on and on about "bulking up for next season," and I was so hungry that I ate over half the pizza that Mary and I both were supposed to split. When I was finishing off one of Mary's pieces, I started to worry that Paul would think I was making a pig of myself, but he and Ian weren't paying any attention to either of us; they were arguing over whether

Golden State or San Antonio were going to win the basketball super bowl or something this year. It was so boring, fortunately they forgot to ask my opinion.

When we got back to my house, Paul walked me to the door, and I wasn't looking forward to that kiss I knew was coming. His face is rough. I can't decide whether he is trying to grow a beard or doesn't know how to shave right. The kiss was about the same as last time (not very good) except that it had the big time smell of pepperoni to it, and I mumbled something like "I had a really good time," and scooted inside the door. Daddy was waiting in his chair and looked at his watch and mumbled something. Mama had already gone to bed, which was a good thing because she can read me like a book and would've known that I had a bad time. I just wanted to go to bed and forget about the whole night.

Chapter Forty-Three: Marcus

Joshua and I got into an argument on Thursday on how the whole blind date thing with Tameka was going to go down. I said I wanted to take her out for pizza after my game Friday night, and he said no, that by the time the game ended and I showered and Coach Henson went over the game, there was no way we could go out for pizza and get Tameka home by her curfew.

Joshua's got me on such a tight chain right now and Jordan is probably playing the big sister role to Tameka, so I had to give in to his way of doing things, which was for him and Jordan to bring Tameka over to our house before the game for a quick meet and greet, and talk about our plans for Saturday night...then let her come see me play and take her home straight after the game.

Really, that wasn't a bad plan, and I've got to tell you that when I saw Tameka—she's a babelicious babe for sure. I just played it cool when Jordan was introducing us, and I made sure when the four of us were going to the game that I asked what Tameka's hobbies and interests were, just stupid stuff like that, so that Joshua and Jordan wouldn't get mad at me from the get-go.

I was so psyched when the game started to show her my skills and to impress her that I couldn't throw it in the ocean. I touched the ball for the first time on our second possession, and I dribbled around behind the line and shot and the ball careened off the backboard, which led to a fast break slam for Woodstock. Next time down, I drove to the hoop but got stripped, and then, maybe, I started pressing a little. I missed a floater in the lane and a jumper from the elbow that I usually make, and then Coach Henson got all bent out of shape and gave me an earful on the bench, which Tameka definitely didn't need to see. I was out of the game for the rest of the first quarter, and when I got back in about five minutes in to the second, I missed a jumper and had a layup blocked and again Henson benched me...this time for the rest of the half. We're down at home, for gosh sakes, by 10 at the half, when we should have put Woodstock away midway through the second quarter.

As I left the court at halftime, I looked up and there was Joshua's leaning over the seats next to the exit ramp, motioning for me to come over to him. I came over and he leaned down to me and says just "play your game, you're too good to be playing like that." I was expecting for him to really yell at me, but actually what he said was pretty good advice. Then when we got into the locker room, Coach Henson said about the same thing...just let the game come to me and "stop pressing."

On our first possession of the second half, Quentin and me got out on a fast break and he gave me a perfect feed, and usually I would just have slammed it home, but this time I just laid it in...the way things had been going I just wanted an easy bucket to get me back in the swing of things. Two possessions later, I made a beautiful finger roll on a give and go, and then Quintin and me got together on another fast break and this time I slammed it home, and the crowd just went wild! We'd cut the lead down to four and all of a sudden I'm feeling it. Woodstock's coach called a time out, but it was too late. On our very next possession, I drained a long three from the top of the key and Woodstock turned it over on the very next possession and Quintin makes them pay with a perfect feed to our center. We're up one, and I canned a jumper and another three and, man, you could see it in the Woodstock players' faces—that they're about to get run out of the gym...warm up the bus, fellows, this game's over. I ended up scoring 22 points in the second half and we won by 15.

The next night, apparently Joshua and Jordan had decided just to keep the date simple—we went out for pizza, then went out to the mall and walked around and had some ice cream and coffee and then called it a night. Tameka, all she wanted to talk about was the game and my sizzling second half, but I felt that Joshua and Jordan were watching my every move and listening to everything I was saying...that Jordan, you can't put anything past her. So I was on my best behavior and kept asking Tameka about her favorite classes and how was school going for her, and what was her school like and what were her hobbies and what did she want to do for a career...just stupid stuff that nobody cares about, but stuff I had to say if there was going to be a second date.

I didn't put any moves on Tameka when I was walking her to the door, just asked her if she had a good time, and she said yes. And then I asked her if she would like to go out again, and she said "definitely yes," so it was a pretty good date and a pretty good weekend. It looks like I've got a brand new girlfriend!

Chapter Forty-Four: Mia

Thursday during math tutoring, I asked Luke if he would like to go to the library to hang out on Saturday, and he gave me a really big smile and said that would be "fantastic." I said I would ask my mama if I could go and asked if he needed to ask his parents. He said they were going to a stock car race for the weekend and were leaving on Friday morning. All he had to do before they came back was wash two cars, and he could get that done Friday after school and Saturday morning before he rode his bike to meet me.

So I told him I would ask Mama Thursday after school and our "date" would be set. As soon as I said the word *date*, I was a little mad at myself because our getting together like that really wouldn't be a date, but I do so very much want to date him next year. I confess that I think about going out with him all the time next fall. He's so sweet to me and we can talk and talk about all kinds of things, and, oh, he's just the type of boy I could fall in love with one day. I know I'm too young to know what love is, and I'm way too young to even think that I definitely know what type of boy would be the right one for me.

But when I look at boys at school and see how they act in class, in the halls, and in the cafeteria, I think I can tell which boys have potential to be really good men one day. Allen is a really nice boy that would make a good husband, but nobody I know is sweeter than Luke. On the other hand, being married to Marcus would be the worst kind of nightmare, the way he is now. It would be like training a cat—impossible.

I want a man that will make me feel safe and secure and will always be faithful to me. I definitely know that much already. I want a guy who will look upon me as a partner and will help take care of the house and not leave all the work to me. Mama expects Poppa to help out around the house; she once told me that he wasn't very good about that when they first married, that she had to "train him." I don't think I would have to train Luke, he would want to help me.

I could see Luke and me coming home from work and him doing the laundry while I was fixing dinner. I really could see that. I know it's silly to think that far ahead in life, but I guess that's what we girls do—think about the future. I don't think most boys do, but I bet Luke does.

So after dinner Thursday evening, when Mama went off to sew in her bedroom and Poppa was watching TV, I knocked on the door and came in and asked if it would be alright if Luke and I met at the library Saturday morning and read and hung out until it closed at 1:00? She frowned and then I hurried on and said that I would ride my bike and she wouldn't have to drive me and waste gas. Mama then said, no, that she would take me and pick me up and that she wouldn't tell Poppa that I was meeting a boy and that she wanted to look this boy over a little when she dropped me off. And I thanked her and thanked her, and she smiled just a little and asked what made Luke so special, and I told her how sweet he was, and that he was smart and would be a success in life, I just knew it. I didn't add that he would do well in something as long as there was absolutely no math involved.

Mama was a little slow leaving the house Saturday morning. I think she was stalling around so that she could make sure that Luke would beat us to the library, so she could look him over really well. Sure enough, Luke was sitting outside the library on a bench when we pulled up and Mama, when she saw him, said, "Well he's cute, I'll give him that." And that made me so happy that she had something positive to say. Luke stood up when I got out of the car. I had told him Friday that Mama was going to drop me off and for him to be on his best behavior, but I didn't really have to worry about him, I knew he would be polite.

Mama called out to us after I got out of the car to "get some good studying done," and actually we were going to work a little on history homework, but I think Mama was just trying to say something. Luke called out "Yes, ma'am," and then Mama drove away. I told him, "Well, now you've met Mama," and he grinned. And I reached out my hand to him, and he smiled again and took it, and we walked up the steps hand-in-hand for just that brief time, and it was just the most wonderful feeling holding hands with him again.

We were at the library for four hours until it closed, and the time just raced by, it was like we were only there 20 minutes. We got the history homework out of the way first thing, then we read *Grapes of Wrath* for a while and talked about it, and the rest of the time we just talked about all kinds of things while we sat side by side at a computer. The most amazing thing that Luke told me was that he had saved almost a thousand dollars from three years of mowing lawns and not eating school lunches this year. That he figured once he had saved $15,000 dollars he would have enough money to buy four or five acres out in the country, that he was 1/15th there, and if he got a job after school next year and the rest of high school and continued to save his money and if he went to college and worked there, by the time he graduated he would have enough money. It was the first time Luke had ever talked about maybe definitely going to college and that made me really happy. Then my imagination really went wild, and I started thinking about living with Luke in a little house out in the country and how wonderful that would be.

It was just a perfect four hours, and Luke and I were outside the library when it was closing and Mama pulled up and Luke said, "Thank you for bringing Mia, ma'am," and waved and said goodbye.

Guy Talk,
Girl Talk

Chapter Forty-Five: Luke

Wednesday, Allen said that Russell had offered to take him trout fishing Saturday morning really early when the fish would be biting, and would I be interested in coming over to spend the night Friday to save time in the morning. I said "Gosh, yeah," Mom and Dad were going out of town Friday night to go pick up a car somewhere, so I knew they wouldn't have any problem with me being gone.

Allen and I haven't talked as much this year as we used to, he's been so busy studying and he hangs out with Paige most every weekend it seems. Usually they just go to her house or his house and watch Netflix and eat pizza. That would be okay to do with a girl, but I can't imagine taking Mia to my house to hang out. Dad would be furious to see a Hispanic person in his house.

Before I walked over to Allen's, I ate dinner alone at my house...the last two deer burgers left from that doe I killed last fall. Mom and Dad weren't too keen on me going hunting last year, but they sure haven't had any problem eating that deer. I'm not even worried about them letting me hunt next year. I'm going to try to kill at least three deer next year with my crossbow.

It didn't take Allen and me long to plan what lures we were going to use on Saturday—Mepps Aglia spinners. Early season stocked rainbow trout will hit them in a heartbeat. We decided we would try to catch at least four or five to eat—

they're really good sprinkled with lemon juice, you know. Allen and I never have done much talking about girls, but I had to ask him what was it like hanging out with Paige, and he said it was great. The only bad thing was that his dad (Allen's parents are divorced) or Paige's mom had to take them everywhere, and it was really embarrassing sitting in the backseat with her and making small talk until they got dropped off at the mall or somewhere. But that was better than not going anywhere at all with her, and after all, what choice did he have until he got his driver's permit.

I had to ask Allen what his favorite kind of date with Paige was, and he first said going to a movie, but then he said maybe going to a coffee house at the mall was pretty good, too…that they would get dropped off there and could talk and hang out and drink coffee for an hour or so, and then go walking around the mall and get some ice cream or something. One time Allen said they were at the mall, and on the spur of the moment, he decided to take Paige to a sweet shop and bought her some dark chocolate truffles, and she got really excited about that. I listened really carefully the whole time he was talking about those dates, because I was thinking I might be able to use some of that information next fall if Mia and I start going out.

Then Allen started teasing me about Mia and said he heard that she and I were "talking," and I said that we were just hanging out, and he said "Yeah, yeah, sure," that I was "sweet on her" and I know I must've got red in the face and finally I said that I liked her a lot, and wanted to go out with her next year because that's when her parents said she could date. Allen next said something like "Everybody knows you two are going to go out next year, it's no secret, it's so obvious that you're both stuck on each other." At first, I got a little mad when he said that, but then I began thinking that Mia must be getting teased too about me, and probably she had told her friends that she liked me. I still have trouble believing that any girl would like-like me, but I guess it's true…it is true, but it's still hard to believe.

Then I asked Allen if he thought maybe we could double date next year, did he think that his father or Russell would mind picking us up, and he said no problem, that double dating would be awesome. That really made me happy because I can't see Dad every driving me up to a Hispanic girl's house and being happy about it, and Mom might be different, but I don't think she'd be too happy about it either…besides they're gone most weekends anyway. So now, I've got two options for us going out next year, Mia and I riding our bikes somewhere to do something and Allen's father or Russell taking us on a double date. This dating thing might work out.

Then Allen and I channel surfed and watched bits and pieces of a couple of NBA games and went to bed. I didn't sleep much all night. I kept waking up thinking about Mia or trout and making just the right cast and then one time I remembered that I had forgotten to put fresh line on my spinning reel, but I figured that these were stocked trout, not river smallmouths, so my line wouldn't break if I got a nice one on…so finally I got some sleep.

The next morning after breakfast and after we got to the creek, Russell said he would fish downstream and let Allen and me fish upstream, which was really nice of him because it's always best to fish for trout by wading upstream and keeping a low profile so they won't spook. The creek was pretty big and wide, so Allen and I didn't have to take turns making casts. It didn't take us long to get into a competition to see who could catch the most trout and be the first to catch our limit of six. I ended up catching my sixth one right after he caught his fifth, so I had bragging rights for the day. But Allen caught his limit right after I did, so things worked out pretty well for us both. We filleted the trout right on the bank, and Allen texted his brother that we were ready to go home, so that the trout wouldn't spoil. I cooked up three of mine for lunch that day when I got home and ate the other three for lunch on Sunday. It was a really good weekend.

Chapter Forty-Six: Elly

I just knew that Paul was going to ask me out again for this weekend. I had put him off last weekend because I told him my family was going to do "family things" all weekend, which really wasn't much of a lie (well, I guess it really was) because our family things consisted of us eating meals and my helping Mom with the weekend laundry and cleaning. All I did last Friday and Saturday nights was read, text, snack, and watch TV.

So Monday before school, I asked Mom if I could have a sleepover party Friday night for my girlfriends, and she said how many, and I said seven or eight and she said okay...that she would buy some pizza and soft drinks, and we could all sleep in the basement and everybody could bring sleeping bags. So I texted Paige, Mary, Kylee, Jayla, and Hannah and met up with Mia and Camilla before school, and everybody said super and that they would ask their moms. By lunchtime Tuesday it was all set, and sure enough Paul came by and did his "let's go get some ice cream routine" but when he asked me out, I told him about the sleepover and said I had family plans for Saturday and maybe some other time. I'll go out with him again, I guess, after all who else is going to go out with me. But not so soon after that last boring date.

Friday night, everybody came over around 6:00 and Mom helped us bring the pizza and soft drinks downstairs, and she said we were on our own... "Enjoy your girl talk." The first 30 minutes all we mostly did was eat pizza and drink diet soft drinks…I don't know how many calories we saved by the diet drinks because all of us had about four or five pieces each, and I confess that I think I had six. After that, the subject quickly turned to boys. Boys that we definitely wanted to date, boys that we might like to date, boys that we would never date, and for those of us who were allowed to date guys, what were their pros and cons.

Then Mary, she's always trying to rile everybody up and start something, bless her, said let's make a list of the ninth grade boys we'd least like to date. Immediately, Kylee and Camila shrieked, looked at each other, and then yelled out at the same time, "Marcus!" And everybody laughed at that, and Hannah said what was his problem and Kylee said, "Marcus being Marcus is Marcus' problem; he's too full of himself and immature," and everybody laughed again; this time it was more like hooting than laughing.

Then Hannah started in on Mia and asked where would she rate Luke on the date or no date list, and all Mia would do was smile in such a sweet, shy way, and that made Hannah just tease her all the more. The more I'm around Mia, the more I like her, the better friends we're becoming. Hannah wouldn't let up and then she said for Mia to tell us "what was up with her and Lucas and 'libraries.'" and Hannah pronounced *libraries* like it was 10 syllables long…she said Luke and her were going to the library three times a week at school, which I knew about, but now they were "seeing each other" on Saturdays at the public library (which I didn't know about) and where were they really going on Saturdays.

All that time Hannah was teasing her, Mia just smiled and looked so happy; it was so obvious that she's really into Luke…that it didn't matter what Hannah or anybody else said. Finally, Hannah said she wasn't going to stop teasing her until Mia said why she liked Luke so much, and you could just see Mia thinking really deeply about that and she said something like, "He's the sweetest boy I've ever met, he cares about what I think and treats me with respect, and we talk about all kinds of things, and he asks my opinion on things, and I just love talking to him and being with him and walking along with him and holding his hand."

There was this long pause after Mia said all that, she was really serious...not joking around like we all were, then Mary said, "You'd better hang on to him then," and this was from Mary who called Luke a ragamuffin at the beginning of the year. Then we were off to another subject. But I kept thinking about what Mia had said. I have to confess that I was envious of her and Luke...Paul has never held my hand when we were walking somewhere, and he's never asked me about what I thought about anything except stupid sports questions and games. So later in the night when we were all getting really sleepy and things were getting quiet and Camila and Paige had already fallen asleep, I walked over to Mia and the two of us went over to the fireplace and just sat and chatted for about 15 minutes.

I told her that I had really enjoyed eating lunch with her on Mondays and Wednesdays and was glad that she and I were becoming better friends and that she was a really sweet person and I was happy that she and Luke looked like they had a relationship with potential. Mia smiled and said that she also was glad to get to know me better and thanked me for the nice comments about her and Luke. She said that Luke had stuttered a lot and was nervous and quiet when she first started talking to him, but then as they had gotten to know each other, that he had stopped stuttering and even told her that when he really liked a girl, he got "all nervous." Then she said that Luke had paid me a compliment one day right after Ms. Hawk had asked the three of us to be on the Yearbook staff next year and work together on assignments...that Luke had said that Mia and I were the two sweetest, nicest girls in the ninth grade, and he liked us both a lot and was looking forward to being on Yearbook staff with us.

It was then that I remembered that night last fall at the football game when Luke was so nervous around me, and all those other times in eighth grade and this year, and then I realized that he may have been that way because he had a crush on me. Right then while Mia was still talking, I tried to imagine what it would be like to date Luke, and I tried to imagine what my parents would think of that…that they probably wouldn't be too happy about it. Finally, I just decided to put any thoughts of Luke and me out of my mind. I had enough to worry about right now. Still, after our talk, I felt a little jealous about Luke and Mia…is it wrong of me to feel that way?

Chapter Forty-Seven: Marcus

Caleb and I haven't had much time lately to do any talking about next year's football season, girls, or school or anything else. He's been dating Leigh since football season ended, so there's that, and, of course, I've had a lot of different girls on my arm, too, all year, so we haven't had much of a chance to connect.

Thursday, Caleb and I started talking during lunch, about our needing to get together and he asked if I'd be interested in riding home with him when his dad picked him up after my game Friday night. I could spend the night at his house, and we could watch Sports Center and an NBA game if a good one was on, and we could catch up a little. That it would be too late for him and Leigh to go out and probably the same would be true with me and Tameka. I didn't want to tell him that I needed permission from my parents to come to his house, so I said no sweat, that he could count on me riding home with him and spending the night. Later, I asked my parents if it would be okay and they said sure. They live in the same neighborhood as we do—he's just six houses down, and I could walk home in the morning.

After Caleb and I went downstairs to his family's rec room, we found a good NBA game on—the Mavs at Golden State—so we settled in to watch that. The first thing Caleb asked me was how many points did I drop Friday night, and I said 24, and he asked next how many treys I drained; it seemed

like five, and I said, no, it was six, and we both laughed at that
…that I was so hot that he could lose count of how many I
poured in. "Man," he said, "you're even better at basketball
than football," that "hoops might be your best sport after all."

I told him that Joshua had been saying the same thing, and
normally, I don't like to admit that my big brother is right
about anything, but maybe he was spot on about the basketball
thing, and what did Caleb really think—should I mostly
concentrate on basketball?

Caleb said, no, no, no, that he needed me as his go-to
receiver next year, and he didn't see any reason in the world
why I couldn't play both sports in high school and at a
university, and if I was a two-sports star, then the recruiters
would be fighting among themselves to offer me scholarships.
Caleb next said maybe I shouldn't go to a school like Alabama
because they usually didn't have much of a basketball team;
maybe I should go to somewhere like Michigan State, or
Florida State would be a good fit, too. I said I wouldn't mind
going to Duke to play hoops, but their football team wasn't any
good, and he agreed that Duke was out because of the football
team not being much.

I asked Caleb what were his workout goals, and he said he
wanted to gain ten pounds of muscle in his upper body and
wanted to add a little more arm strength, but he really didn't
think he needed much else—except for a better offensive line
for next year. We both laughed at that, and, man, we both
agreed that our offensive line sucked last year, that Paul, Ian,
and Richard especially needed to bulk up and start playing with
more intensity, but that we didn't know if those upper classmen
had it in them.

I had to ask him about Leigh, and he said she was super-
hot, and those long legs of hers just drove him wild, and we
both laughed at that, too. I said every one of my dates all year
had been with Joshua and Jordan in the car, and I was sort of

not so down with that anymore, because Jordan was super controlling and Joshua was always ready to butt in on my business, but it was still better than sitting in the backseat with some girl and one of my parents or the girl's mother or father driving and dropping us off somewhere. It was about that time that I brought up the subject of maybe me and Caleb doing some double dating; his mom has a van and maybe we could work out some sort of arrangement where Tameka's parents dropped her off at my house, and then Caleb's mom picked us up after she had picked up Leigh.

Caleb said that would be awesome, and we maybe could go out to a swanky restaurant next Saturday night and show Leigh and Tameka what it's like to date future pro athletes. All of that just sounded great to me, and I said I was down with it and that my parents gave me money to go out anywhere I wanted, and it would be great not to have Joshua and Jordan watching my every move for a change.

We then got serious about watching the game, and we watched Steph Curry just absolutely demolish the Mavs in the second half, and Caleb said I had a game that was very similar to Curry's, and I agreed. I'm going to keep that two-sport thing in college in mind.

Chapter Forty-Eight: Mia

Earlier in the week, Elly asked me to come to a sleepover at her house Friday night, and I was so excited that she would invite me and said that I would ask my mama. Mama said that would be fine, but she wanted me to understand first that Elly's neighborhood was a lot nicer than ours and that Elly's family would have a lot of things that we didn't have, but that was okay, and I was not to be envious.

I said I understood that, but Mama wasn't quite satisfied yet. She said she wanted to emphasize that we were not lower class, that thanks to my grandparents' hard work and hers and Poppa's, we had moved up a lot, but we still would never have the things that Elly's family did but maybe one day I would. I asked Mama what class we were in, and she paused and thought a while and said, to be exact, she would classify us as lower middle class and the houses in Elly's neighborhood were all upper class ones, though some were still considerably nicer than others. Again, I said I understood all that, and Mama said she had so many dreams for me and my future and the man I would marry and the job I would have. I think all that is one of the reasons she seems so cold to the idea of Luke and me being such good friends, besides him not being Hispanic...that his neighborhood is about like ours. She doesn't know him like I do, though, and she doesn't see the potential that he has.

I was the first one to arrive at Elly's house—Mama never wants me to be late for anything—so Elly took me upstairs to see her bedroom and gave me a tour. Her bedroom is almost bigger than our living room, and her house is like three of ours. The backyard was just huge, but there wasn't a garden or chicken run back there, though there was plenty of room for things like that. Her mama has a space for a flower garden, but it's much smaller than ours.

While I was thinking about all that wasted space, I remembered something else that Mama had told me. That you can't always measure success by the size of a house or a person's possessions. You measure it by how you feel about yourself and what you have accomplished...that you can find joy in many things that don't have anything to do with money. Mama and I get a lot of joy from our chickens and flower garden. All I saw in Mia's backyard was mostly grass. With a backyard that big, she could have a goat or two and definitely chickens.

After we ate dinner, all the girls wanted to do was talk about boys, and I knew that it wouldn't be long before they started teasing me about Luke. Hannah and Mary were worse than anyone, I think everybody except Elly got in a few comments about him. But I didn't mind. I would rather go with Luke to the library or go ride bikes with him (maybe we can do that some this spring) than go out to an expensive restaurant with somebody that I don't much like. Camila and Kylee are good examples of that when they went out with Marcus to all those nice places, but they didn't have a good time or even get to know Marcus better.

The highpoint of my evening was sitting by the fireplace and talking to Elly after people had started to get tired and fall asleep. She asked a lot of questions about Luke, and we talked a lot about all kinds of things. I asked her if she needed any help with fixing breakfast for everybody in the morning, that I was used to getting up early and would be glad to help her. Elly said that she had just assumed that her mom was going to cook for everyone, but now she realized, thanks to me, that it would be not be treating her mother right to put that burden on her. So Elly said that she would set the alarm on her phone, and we would cook up something for everybody…that she would text her mom now so that she would know not to get up early the next morning. I asked her if her mama had any salsa and cilantro, and Elly said she was sure her mom did, and I said great, we would cook Mexican baked eggs.

The next morning, I was already awake when Elly came over to get me up. We had the best time talking while we were cooking for everybody. I asked Elly if she really liked Paul, and she said not really, that going out with him was just something to do, that they had had only two dates, but she knew that he was going to ask her out again for this coming weekend and she had just about run out of excuses on why she couldn't go out with him, so she was going to say yes for this Friday or Saturday night, whichever one he wanted—it didn't matter to her; going out would at least get her out of the house.

We then started talking about what we wanted to do with our lives, and Elly said that she could imagine becoming a teacher, and I told her that she would be awesome at that. Then she said she would like to live in a big, nice house like her parents, but then I could tell that she thought she had hurt my feelings because my family doesn't have a nice house like hers. But she shouldn't have thought that, it didn't hurt my feelings. I tried to smooth things over by saying that I would like a nice house like that, too, but what I would really like to do was live out in the country on some land, so I could have a really big flower garden and a huge vegetable garden and chickens and maybe a goat. I didn't add that I dreamed sometime of living like that with Luke, but I think about that a lot.

She asked what I wanted to do, and I said sometimes I wanted to become a nurse like Mama, but more and more, I thought I might want to become a doctor, that I would enjoy working with little kids and keeping them healthy. I knew doing all that would be expensive, but maybe I could get scholarships. I want to get together with Elly again soon. Maybe her parents would let her come to my house.

Testing Stress

Chapter Forty-Nine: Luke

It's spring and that means state testing, and Mrs. Burkhead was all in a hissy fit Monday about our biology standardized test on Thursday. I wasn't worried about it; I know that biology stuff, I really enjoy going out in the woods with field guides and learning about trees, fish, birds, and all kinds of wild animals and plants. I keep a list of every bird I have identified in our area, and I've got about 115 on the list and that includes the ones that just breed here in the summer and overwinter here. It's fascinating, but I can't stand how Mrs. Burkhead teaches.

She spent the whole period Monday lecturing, and my mind drifted in and out, but mostly out. At the end of the period, she made three announcements. One was that she was going to give Pizza Hut coupons worth 15, 10, and 5 dollars for the students who had the three top scores on the standardized test; two, that if the whole class passed we would have a pizza party, and third, that three other poor suckers and I had to stay after class to talk with her. I knew, everybody in class knew, that she was singling us out for our bad grades, and I just knew she was going to assign us to after school tutoring. It was humiliating. She shouldn't have announced our names like that; she should have caught us on the way out or something— anything to keep from embarrassing us like that.

So after class, there we were the four dunces in front of Mrs. Burkhead's desk, and sure enough, she said it was mandatory that we come to after school tutoring with her on

Wednesday and Thursday, and that our parents would have to provide for a way home for us. I told her, and it was the truth, that I worked at my father's used car lot after school, and I was sorry but I couldn't stay, that Dad had bought two cars over the weekend, and I had to clean them up by the end of the week. Mrs. Burkhead got really mad and said that "indeed" I was staying after school, and again I said I couldn't, and out came the discipline referral sheets from her right upper drawer just like all those other times this year. That woman's got a hair trigger temper. She was so mad her hand was shaking, and she was circling a whole bunch of things on the sheet she was filling out for me...so off I went to Mr. Caldwell's office.

He wasn't happy to see me, but I get this real feeling that he's not too happy about Mrs. Burkhead either, he's never criticized her in front of me...but still, I can't shake the feeling that there's friction between them. I told Mr. Caldwell what had happened, that I was telling the truth about my not being able to stay after school, and that I knew what my strengths and weaknesses were in biology, that there was no way I was going to score below the 400 passing marker, that I wasn't going to score a perfect 600 either, but I would do all right. I just needed to study the boring stuff like fungi and microscopic things.

Mr. Caldwell was nodding his head, and I could tell he was thinking about something, and then he asked about how long was I going to need to study those topics, and I said about two hours. And he said, "Good, I'm assigning you to two days of in-school suspension during biology class. You can work on the things you need to brush up on then."

I thanked and thanked him for kicking me out of class for two days...two whole days without Mrs. Burkhead and her smart mouth...it was like going on a vacation...and I promised Mr. Caldwell that I would ace the biology test. He smiled at me and said he agreed that I would and added that it was a "win-

win-win" situation for me, Mrs. Burkhead, and him. After all, I couldn't be kicked out of her class if I wasn't there.

I spent those two periods studying really hard, even though I would have preferred reading *Grapes of Wrath*. Both Mia and I are almost done, it's an awesome book. On Thursday, I took the test; it was really easy and I already knew most of the stuff from my wandering around outside and looking things up online that I didn't know, plus I had read up on the fungi and crap, so I knew about that, too.

I was back in class on Friday, and Mrs. Burkhead announced that next Thursday the scores would be back, and "expedited retakes" would be the following Thursday and she stared right at me when she said that. I lowered my head when she did that. I knew she was just looking for an excuse to write me up again. What was it going to be this time, you old hag, "Luke looked at me wrong," was that what you were going to write down?

Thursday the scores came back, and when I got my results back, it showed that I had scored a 578. Mrs. Burkhead announced that everybody had passed and that we would have a pizza party on Friday like she promised. I got to thinking about those Pizza Hut coupons and how I could sell mine if I had one of the three best scores and make some money to put in my banking account. So I raised my hand and she kept ignoring me. Then I turned around and begged Mia to ask her who had the three top scores, so Mia did, and then a bunch of other kids started begging for the three top scorers to be announced.

Old Mrs. Burkhead couldn't back down from that, and she said that Elly had been the third highest scorer and Mia the second, and then she mumbled out that my score was the highest. Son of a gun! When I went up to her desk, I started to say something smart like, "I couldn't have done it without you, Mrs. Burkhead." But Mia has been sort of working on me not to do things like that, and I just gave Mrs. Burkhead a big smile. By the end of the next class, I had an extra 15 dollars in my pocket, and that money was on its way to the bank. It was a really good day.

Chapter Fifty: Elly

When Mrs. Burkhead announced that the biology state tests would be Thursday and there would be prizes for the best three scores, Mia came up to me after class and asked if I wanted to come over to her house after school on Wednesday (I could ride her bus home with her). have dinner with her family, and we could study before and after dinner. That she had been wanting to repay me for my inviting her over to the sleepover, that her parents always said she should respond that way when someone did something nice for her. She said it had only taken her about an hour to walk home from my house after the sleepover, and we could time our studying to make sure that I got home before dark.

I had no idea that Mia had walked home after the sleepover, I had just assumed that her parents came to get her. I remembered her saying that her father works on Saturdays; does her family only have one car? Dad says we need three, one each for Mom and him, and the jeep for when he goes on fishing trips or when the weather is bad. Dad says he will buy me a car when I get my license, but it will be a used one because I'm bound to put some "dings" on it, he said.

I told Mia I would text my mom to see if I could, and Mom texted back before school ended and said that was fine. When I got off the bus, I was surprised at how small the house was and how little the backyard was. Her parents weren't home from work yet, and Mia said she had to do her chores really

quickly before we started studying, and would I mind helping.
Of course I said I would be glad to help, and Mia said great;
would I mind checking to see if her hens had laid any eggs?
Meanwhile she would start her sisters on their homework…
that it was her parents' rule that her sisters Isabella and Emma
start their homework as soon as they got home from school.
Her parents must be strict.

Mia handed me an egg basket and pointed to the backyard,
and I went out the backdoor and started looking for the eggs.
The hens saw me and got scared and ran inside their house, and
the rooster just stared at me and gave me this evil look and
then he crowed, like he was saying "Get out of my yard!" I
didn't see any eggs anywhere in the yard, and the rooster
looked so angry I was afraid to open the door of the henhouse,
and he crowed twice in a row and stared at me again. I went
back inside the house and told her I was afraid of the rooster
and the hens were afraid of me, and I didn't see any eggs in the
yard.

Mia started laughing so hard that she couldn't stop, and I
kept saying "What, what, what." Finally she said that the eggs
would be in the nesting boxes inside the henhouse, and she
would pick up Mr. Macho and hold him while I got the
eggs…that he wouldn't bite, but he "didn't like strangers being
around his hens." Mr. Macho had once bitten off the head of a
garter snake that had come into the yard, and all the cats in the
neighborhood were scared of him, she said.

I went inside the henhouse and there was chicken poop all
over the floor, and it was gross, but I found six eggs in the
boxes, and I've got to say that it was exciting to be gathering
them. I mean, I know that chickens lay eggs—duh—but to
think that those chickens in that yard had laid those eggs, and
Mia's family was going to eat those eggs instead of supermarket
ones…well, that was kind of neat. Oh, and one of the eggs I
picked up, a hen was sitting on the nest when I came up to it,

and she left an egg behind when she hopped up, and the egg was still warm. That egg must just have come out of her...wow!

Not long after my chicken egg and rooster adventure was over, Mia's parents came home and Mia's mom told her that she didn't have to help with dinner that night, for us to go study. I asked Mia if she helps with dinner every night, and she said some nights it was her chore to cook dinner for everybody, but most nights she just helped her mama. It made me think that I rarely cooked dinner at my house, and most nights I didn't even help Mom...maybe I should start doing that.

I was really hoping for Mexican-type dishes for dinner, but Mia's mom served hamburgers and French fries for dinner with vanilla pudding for dessert. Mia's dad was really quiet during dinner; I think he seemed nervous that I was there. When we finished eating and went off to her room, I was surprised how small it was. The room was very clean and neat and everything was in its place...not like mine which is, like, a disaster area except on weekends when I have to clean it up.

I had to ask Mia if they often ate Mexican foods, and she looked a little embarrassed and said, "Poppa insisted that Mama serve American food in honor of you being here." She said sometimes they had a traditional Mexican dinner, sometimes they had both American and Mexican dishes, but she couldn't ever remember a meal like this one...that her "poppa had acted very strange" when I asked if I could come over, but she then added that he was glad Mia was paying me back for her coming to my house.

We studied our biology notes for about an hour; we really didn't need to work that long. We both knew just about everything that was probably going to be on the test. About the time we thought we had studied long enough, my mom knocked on the door and it was time for me to go. I'm not worried about the big biology test.

Chapter Fifty-One: Marcus

I did okay on the big state tests on biology and math, making a 412 and 418 on them. I'm getting a *B* or a *C* in both classes, and no D-I school is going to have any problems with those scores and my grades. But a couple of days after the scores came out, when I got home my parents said they wanted to talk to me...alone...after dinner. I could tell by their tone that they had an attitude about something.

Sure enough, after dinner, they told Joshua that they wanted to talk to me alone, and he gave me one of those "I told you so" smirks that he always gives and left the dining room in a hurry. I think he enjoys seeing me get in trouble, although this time I really had no idea what my parents would be so bent out of shape about. Mom said that I had not told them what my scores on the state tests were, so she called the guidance department and found out and that she and Dad were not satisfied with my scores or my grades in my classes. I got angry and told them that both my grades and scores were fine, that I would have time to make even better grades now that basketball season was over. I averaged 20 points per game and the local paper named me "freshman of the year" for our conference. We didn't make the playoffs because Quintin didn't get me the ball enough in our conference tournament, but, outside of that, things have been going really well for me lately. My parents need to get off my back about this silly stuff.

But when I told them that, they both got really mad, especially Dad. He asked what was my "backup plan" in case I didn't become a pro football and basketball player, like I was "always saying" that I would be. I told him I didn't need a backup plan because I'd already figured everything out and for them just to chill and let me handle my life.

Dad just erupted like a volcano when I said that, and Mom made no effort to calm him down. She was just sitting there at the kitchen table and gritting her teeth. Dad then dropped the grounded bomb on me and said I would not be allowed to go out on dates or over to friends' houses until I had at least a B average in all my classes. I told him that Tameka and I were supposed to have a date Friday night, and Mom said that I could call or text her with the bad news, that I wouldn't be seeing her for a while until my grades improved. I told them that I only had a C average in English, biology, and history, that Ms. Hawk was a terrible teacher and counted off too many points on my papers. I said that history took up too much of my time as it was with all that reading, and I had already passed the state biology test...so what was the big problem.

Dad just shook his head, ran his finger through his hair, and then all of a sudden, he just slammed the table with his fist, and said he was tired of "my mouth and immaturity," that their decision was final regarding my grounding, and that next year, there would be no new car for me to drive when it was time for me to get my license if my grades and attitude didn't show "marked improvement" this spring. I started to snap right back at him, but he was staring right at me, like he was just daring me to open my mouth...then Mom told me to go to my room for the evening...that "this discussion is over."

When I went upstairs, there was Joshua standing in the stairwell. He must have been listening to everything and he said something like, "I warned you, you'd better grow up." And I swear, I was about to belt him in that big gut of his, but then I remembered the last time we got into a fight, which was about three years ago, and he beat the snot out of me. So I decided I'd better not mess with him…he's always been bigger than I am. That's going to change one day when I give him a big time beat down.

I texted Tameka that our date for the weekend was cancelled because I had some flu symptoms, that I didn't want to give the bug to her…that we'd go out again when I was up to par. It won't take me long to bring up my grades. I can make a cheat sheet for the next history quiz; I'm only a few points from a *B* anyway, it will be no sweat to bring up my grades there, and I'm even closer to a *B* in biology. English might still be a problem with all those papers, but I can get Mom to look over my next one…that'll show her that I'm serious about my work and she'll correct most of my errors anyway. I'll be back in business in no time.

Chapter Fifty-Two: Mia

Luke was so worried about the math state test Thursday afternoon that we spent all of our lunch periods Tuesday and Thursday in the library going over possible problems and the review sheet that the teacher had given him. He's so sweet, and I feel so bad for him. He just doesn't understand math, and I want to help him so much, but he just tenses up whenever we go over some of the harder stuff. I just want to give him a big hug and tell him everything will be all right.

In his remedial math class, Luke said they just started in on the Algebra lessons the second semester, and he's so bad at it, I'm not even sure he knows what Algebra is. I mean he doesn't even know the basic information. He said his math grade has dropped from a high D to a low one recently, and it seems like I'm helping him more than ever, and still he's just barely passing for this nine weeks.

Toward the end of the lunch period, when I had time to go over the most important equations one last time, I realized there was no way he was going to pass the test. And I think he realized it, too. He just sighed when I said good luck, and right then I wanted to kiss him for the first time. But I didn't want our first kiss to be in the library and when he was going to take a standardized test in a few minutes.

More and more, I've been thinking about our first date next year when we're sophomores and our first kiss. I want both to be special. I know he's going to ask me out, and I know

I'm going to say yes. What I don't know is where we will go on our first date and how Mama and Poppa will feel about it, and how we will get to wherever we will go. I would be happy riding our bikes somewhere and having a picnic; we wouldn't need any money to have a good time together. Just being with him and talking about things would be enough for me...and I think for Luke, too.

The bell rang for lunch to be over, and I squeezed Luke's hand, and he squeezed mine, too, and I told him to meet me at the entranceway of the school before we got on our buses, to let me know how he thought he did. He said he would. When I saw him at the end of the day, he looked so gloomy, and he said the whole test had been a disaster. He said he got so nervous, and it seemed like he was taking too much time on the questions; they were all multiple choice, but Luke called them "multiple guess."

Luke said with about 20 questions left on the test, the problems got harder than ever, and everything that we had drilled about went "right out" of his head, so he just decided to "Christmas tree" those last 20 questions. He penciled in A, B, C, D, and then did D, C, B, A, until the test was over, and turned in his test and left.

I had taken my math state test that morning and felt like I had done really well. When my scores for my class came back a week later, I had made a 578, which was about what I thought I had made...some of the problems were really hard, so I had felt like I had missed a few of them. Since my scores came back for my honors Algebra I class, I knew Luke's must have come back too, so I could hardly wait until we met in the library to see if maybe he had gotten lucky and passed.

When I entered the library, Luke was already sitting at what we call "our computer," and I hurried over to him and he saw me and gave me the biggest smile. He said he had passed with a 405, that "Christmas treeing" over those last 20 problems must have turned out okay. I was so happy for him that I gave him the biggest hug right there in the library. I don't care who saw us. Later when I thought about Luke passing that test, I sort of had doubts about the whole system of those state math tests. I mean if Luke, who is just absolutely horrible in math, could pass the test by just pure luck, really now, how valid could those tests be. Of course, if he had failed the test, that wouldn't have been good, either. At least, state testing is over for the spring.

Nights
of
Magic
(Or Not)

Chapter Fifty-Three: Luke

Thursday during lunchtime in the library, Mia came up to me with a very serious look on her face and said she had an idea. Since there's only a few weeks left before the end of school, not much has been happening in math class and she hasn't had to tutor me as much. As bad as I am in math, I've been able to figure out that I've mathematically clinched passing for the year. All that's left now is to determine whether I have a low, middle, or high D...so like who cares a whoop about that. I don't figure they'd fail me for math anyway now since I passed the standardized test. Nobody in the guidance department in their right minds would want me retaking a math class where I've already passed the standardized test. I mean I could be 20 years old and still sitting in ninth grade math...who wants to risk that.

So Mia said for the past week or so, she'd been thinking about this idea she had that involved the two of us, and she had finally gotten up enough nerve to talk to her parents about it, and they said they thought it was a really good idea. I couldn't imagine what kind of idea that would be involving me and told her that, but I was all ears.

Mia said she had thought of a way that we could both make money for college and help each other at the same time. She's been talking more and more about her going to college, and I know she is, I bet she wins a scholarship somewhere. I'm not even totally sure I'm going, but I haven't told her that. I guess I will go. Anyway, she said her idea was for us to go into business together as L&M Lawn Mowing and Babysitting, Incorporated. That she had already been "playing" with how the website would look, and because neither one of our families can afford for us to have cellphones, she talked her parents into buying a cheap answering machine that would have a recording telling callers to leave a message and telling how they could e-mail her or me as well if they needed our services. Mia's family has a computer, and so does mine, so we were good to go in that department.

I was amazed at how much time she had spent thinking about this, but she wasn't done yet with her ideas. She said most of the people she babysat for in her neighborhood didn't have enough money to hire me to mow their lawns, but that the people I mowed lawns for had enough money to hire her to babysit. That after school we could visit those families on our bikes, talk about giving them "reduced rates" if they hired both of us to take care of their lawns and babysitting. And we could ask those same people if they could recommend friends and neighbors who likewise could be in need of our services. We could also, over a series of nights, ride up and down middle and upper class neighborhoods and offer people our services.

I kept saying "Wow, I like it," to everything she said, and she still wasn't done with her ideas. She said by us going in together like that we could really expand our business and maybe be booked up almost every day of the summer with my mowing and every night with her babysitting. Mia said her poppa really liked another one of her ideas…it was for her to receive 5% of my lawn mowing check if she found a babysitting client of hers that needed my services, and I would receive 5% of her babysitting check if the reverse happened. Of course, she said she emphasized only the first part of the deal to her poppa, which is why he probably liked it so much.

Finally, Mia suggested that we not call any of my current and possible future clients about this idea, that instead we drop by after school to talk to them. That it would be harder to turn us down if the people were talking to us in person, and we could come dressed in our best pairs of jeans or shorts and looking "all professional," she said. Gosh, this girl is smart, I never would have thought of any of that. She said we could start tonight if I wanted, her parents had given her permission to ride her bike or walk anywhere she needed to go if it had to do with her business, and she asked if I needed to ask my parents about her idea, and I said no…that they would be down with my hustling around making money because Dad certainly knew how to do that.

That night, we went to the neighborhood where Elly, Marcus, Caleb, and a bunch of people that go to our school live. We stopped at Elly's house first because we've both already been there, and Elly's dad really liked the idea of my mowing for him when I brought it up, but said he couldn't see a need for Mia to babysit because Elly could do that. Mia said she understood and asked Elly's mom if she could recommend somebody in the neighborhood that might need both our services. Elly's mom said yes and whipped out her cellphone and called Caleb's house right then. While it was ringing, she said Caleb had two young sisters in elementary school and that she was good friends with Caleb's mom and would talk to her about hiring us as a package deal. That was really nice of her to do that, and after a few minutes of her talking to Caleb's parents, and then Elly's mom handing the phone to Mia to let her explain what the deal was, L&M was good to go at the Caleb household. We headed there next to seal the deal and for us to book times to mow and babysit.

Then we were off to the next place. We had time to visit about eight houses in Elly's neighborhood before the sun started to go down and we had to quit so that Mia could get home before dark. But we booked five mowing jobs for me, and four babysitting ones for Mia. This is going to work out big time.

Chapter Fifty-Four: Elly

The other night, right before Mom and I were going to go to the mall to shop for my prom dress (yes, I'm going to the prom as a freshman…with Paul…he asked me when there was just two weeks to go), I went to answer the doorbell, and to my big surprise there were Mia and Luke standing there. They wanted to talk to my parents about their new mowing and babysitting business. Later, I was really surprised when Dad said he would pay Luke to mow his lawn, because I know he has negative feelings about Luke and his family. After Luke left, Dad told Mom that it was good that Luke was developing some "work skills," that his hiring Luke would "hopefully keep the boy off the welfare rolls." I didn't like what Dad said, I don't think Luke is going to be a failure in life at all.

I've got to admit that I was excited about going to prom, not with Paul, but just to go. I mean how many freshmen girls get a chance to go to prom. Mom and I had the best time picking out a prom dress for me. Finally we chose a cobalt blue gown that showed just a hint of cleavage (which is one of my good parts). The gown has a flowy chiffon skirt that does a pretty good job of hiding two of my worst parts (my butt and thighs).

When prom night finally came…Oh, yes, I really enjoyed Mom fussing over my hair and makeup and getting everything just right…I've got to admit that it was really special to see Paul and Ian and Mary pull up to our house to pick me up. Paul came in to get me and Dad said I could stay out to midnight just this once, and Paul said "thank you, sir," or something like that.

When we got down to the car, Mary just looked super with her long brown hair braided, and just the right amount of blush on her cheeks. I don't think Mom put enough on mine. When I got into the car, that was when the magic for the night sort of ended. Apparently, Paul and Ian had been involved in a loud argument before I got in (at least, that's what Mary told me later) about who had "bulked up the most" since the spring weight lifting had started. That discussion continued after I got in and on our way to the restaurant for dinner.

On the way there, we stopped at a stoplight at the local Dairy Queen, and there were Luke and Mia again, sitting on a bench. They must have been coming back from one of their mowing and babysitting jobs because I saw their bikes parked behind them. Anyway, while we were sitting at the stoplight and waiting for it to turn, I saw Mia tell Luke something, and he laughed; and then he told her something, and she laughed, and the whole time they were holding hands while they were sitting there, eating ice cream cones with their other hands. And I started thinking how romantic and sweet that was and how, meanwhile, Paul and Ian had finished up with the bulking up discussion and moved on to some other sport, was it football or basketball or maybe it was the baseball season…I don't know, I don't care…and I thought that I would rather be eating a two-dollar ice-cream cone with a boy that I liked, than all fancied up and going out to dinner and a prom with a guy who bores me.

Dinner was great, I had flounder and potato croquettes while Mary had salmon and rice. The guys, of course, had huge steaks with baked potatoes and all the extras. Then they both insisted that we have dessert, and I really was too full to eat anymore but Paul insisted, so I had cheese cake and so did Mary. Ian and Paul each had some sort of monstrosity called "death by chocolate" or something, it was huge. I think I've gained five pounds since I've been dating him. I'm not sure because I haven't weighed recently, I'm afraid to. My clothes feel a little tighter. That was the only good thing about Paul waiting so late to ask me out, at least my prom dress still fit right. I really feel that I looked as good as I could have.

When we got to the prom, it was nice, I have to admit. The decorations were beautiful, the juniors did a good job and the snacks were good, too. Paul kissed me twice while we were dancing but around 10:30, he started hanging out with the other football guys, which was fine with me. Honestly, I don't remember a whole lot about what went on. I was tired and bored and ready to go home pretty early on. I really didn't feel comfortable among all those juniors and seniors. When Mary and I went to the restroom to freshen up, Mary said she felt the same way about being around the upperclassmen as I did.

Finally around 11:30, it was time to go home, so we left. When we got home, Paul and I sat in the front seat and made out for a while...I guess it is a requirement after prom. I felt nothing, it was nothing special, while Ian and Mary did the same making out in the backseat. The whole time Paul and I were making out, I kept thinking about Luke and Mia at the Dairy Queen.

Thinking about them instead of the guy I was with, made me think that maybe I've grown up some this year. If someone had asked me a year ago, when I was an eighth-grader, if I would have been thrilled to go to the prom as a freshman, I would have screamed out yes. Now, I'm starting to realize that there are other things about a guy that are more important than him just having a car. I bet I won't be going to the prom next year as Paul's date, at least I hope not. I don't care if I go again until I'm a junior; I just hope if I do go, it's with somebody I really like.

Chapter Fifty-Five: Marcus

My grades have really come up, so my parents have finally laid off with the nagging all the time about how low my averages have been. I started doing my Honors English homework, so my grade there is up to a B. I had a solid B in Algebra I and now it's up to an A; I'm a whiz at math. Of course, I had an A in gym, and I was already making a B in just about everything else. I've had these great cheat sheets in World History the last three tests, and I'm working on another one for when we have our big nine weeks test in two weeks. When I'm done making it, I'm going to take a picture of it with my phone, then during the test, I'll keep my phone between my legs, and look down there when I can't remember something. Mr. Foster doesn't have a clue about what I've been doing.

So with me being back in the good graces of my parents, I'm back in business in the social scene. Caleb and me are both dating ninth grade girls, so obviously we can't take them to prom. We got together the other day and decided that maybe we could have our own little celebration on prom night and have the girls over to one of our houses for food, and video games, and maybe some movies or something.

We had a long conversation about which house we would entertain the girls at, so we started ragging each other about who had the bigger flat screen TV. Ours is a 55 class, and his is only a 40, so guess who won that battle. I told my mom that we wanted pizzas and Edy's Moose Tracks for dinner, and she was down with that because of all my good grades. It's good being back in her good graces; Dad seemed suspicious that my grades have come up so much, especially in history, but like they say, what you don't know, won't hurt you. I don't mind not having to rely on Joshua for wheels and not being around that foul wench Jordan is always a good thing. Mom said she would be glad to pick up Tameka and Leigh if their parents would bring them home, so everything was set up nicely.

Tameka got here first, so I showed her around the house and especially my bedroom where all my trophies are going all the way back to when I was a kid. She seemed really interested in my telling her how I had won all those awards. She already knows about my plans to play D-I football and basketball. I don't know if we'll still be dating then. I don't want to tie myself down before I get to experience college.

After Caleb and Leigh arrived, we all went down to our rec room, and feasted on pizza. Caleb and me probably ate a whole one each, they were so good, and the ice cream was great, too. Caleb and me then played Madden NFL while the girls did some silly game on Playstation. I really wasn't paying attention to what they were doing. I whipped Caleb's butt while we were playing Madden. I mean, I've been on a roll lately.

After it got dark, the four of us went out the rec room door and walked around the backyard for a while, to have some alone time…if you know what I mean. Tameka is way hotter than Camila and Kylee ever were. I can't believe I ever wasted my time and money on them. I've got to tell you I like not having my girlfriend go to the same school as I do. If I meet, like, a hot new transfer girl next year or run into a babe at Mom and Dad's club, I can lay out my charm without Tameka knowing about it and getting in my business.

The NBA playoffs were on when we came back inside, and Caleb and I asked the girls if they minded if we watched some hoops and they said they didn't care. I really need to be studying the moves of those NBA shooting guards. It just dawned on me a couple of weeks ago that I could be playing in the NBA in no more than seven years, less if I turn pro early. If I went pro after my freshman year in D-I, I could be playing pro just four years from now, so I've got to be ready when that time comes.

Caleb knows how much I want to play pro hoops, so he has stopped telling me just to concentrate on football. I appreciate him not wanting me to play just football; I can be his go-to receiver the next three years and fill up the basket in the winter.

Round about 11:00, Tameka's and Leigh's dads showed up. Tameka's old man sort of has this foul expression when he's around me, and he was the same way when he picked her up. I could care less, things are going my way.

Chapter Fifty-Six: Mia

Luke and I are making tons of money with our new business. I'm babysitting every Friday and Saturday night, and one Saturday, I got two jobs, one from 4:30 to 6:30 (a couple with a newborn baby wanted a quick evening out) and the other from 7:00 to 10:00. Several times, I've even gotten to babysit for a couple hours after school for couples who had a special birthday or anniversary night out. Poppa and Mama don't mind driving to get me when it's that late because they know I'm earning money for college. And they know I'll keep my studies up even if I have to go out at night. Luke's mowing somebody's lawn every day after school, which has forced him to have to do his father's used car washing and vacuuming before school.

I'm doing all of the scheduling of our jobs. I've made an Excel spreadsheet on my family's computer that helps me keep track of everything. This past Saturday, I looked over the schedule and didn't see how we could get it all done. Luke had to mow four lawns and one of the couples wanted him to clip all their shrubbery and weed their garden. That same couple wanted me to babysit their two kids from 4:30 to 7:00. So I decided to schedule that family last and told Luke I would take care of the shrubbery and garden from 3:30 to 4:30, and he could get there later and mow the lawn while I was babysitting. Then we could just ride our bikes home from there. Luke trusts me to do the scheduling right, so he was okay with my plan.

It was a really hot day, and I got just filthy doing all of the outside work. It was still really hot when he finished mowing around 7, and the couple came back at the same time from their night out. So we decided to ride our bikes part of the way back home together. We had gone just a little ways when Luke said we were going to take a detour. I followed him for about 20 minutes and then he pulled in to the Dairy Queen parking lot. He grinned and said he was going to treat me to an ice cream cone. My hair was a mess, and I had bits and pieces of shrubbery in it, and I was streaming with sweat from the bike ride, and Luke looked even worse…he had the dirt and grime of four lawns on him. But I was so glad to be with him that I didn't care how I looked.

I was so hungry that I ordered two scoops of chocolate for my cone, then I felt a little guilty about that, about spending so much of Luke's money, and started to tell the lady just one scoop, and Luke said no, it was a two-scoop day for us both, and he ordered a vanilla cone and he said he would pay for both of ours. We sat down on a bench outside the Dairy Queen, and he held my hand and I squeezed his and he squeezed back and though I was so dirty and sweaty, I felt like a princess out on the town. I started to eat my cone really slowly because I just wanted to make the night last as long as I could.

Then I got a little silly and said to Luke, "Since you're paying for my ice cream, is this our first date?" As soon as I said that, I wished I hadn't because it made me look too forward and Mama has told me never to be that way with boys. I mean I'm almost positive that he is going to ask me out for a date next year when my parents said I could date, and I am positive that I'm going to say yes. There's nobody at school I want to go out with except him, he is so sweet and kind and good. I think Mama might be okay with us going out. I worry a lot about Poppa not liking it, but maybe he can meet Luke this spring or summer on one of our jobs and see what a good person he is and how right he is for me.

Luke didn't say anything for a few seconds after I said that, and I began to really worry that I really had been too forward. I was just starting to apologize when he said that he had been thinking a whole lot about asking me out on a date next year, about how to do it because he had never asked a girl out before, and where we could go, and what we would do on our date if I said yes. He made me so happy when he said all that, that I just had to give him a hug, and he grinned and said that he would take that as a yes and would I like to know what he was thinking about where we might go.

Of course, I said yes to all that, and he said he thought that it would be nice for us to go on a picnic on the first Saturday after our first week of being back in school as sophomores, since my parents said I could date my sophomore year. Luke said we could ride our bikes to the national forest that morning and park them back in the woods a ways so that nobody could see them. Then we would go hiking back into the mountains for about a mile or so…he knew a great trail…and we could stop at a beautiful waterfall where a creek flowed near the path and have a picnic there. That I could decide what to pack for the picnic or he could bring his pack fly rod, and he could catch trout for our lunch. If I wanted, he could even show me how to cast a fly rod (it wasn't hard, he said) and maybe I could catch my first fish on our first date.

It was so obvious that he had thought so much about our dating, and it just made me so, so happy that I wanted to give him our first kiss right then, but then I thought that would make me look too forward again, so I didn't. But I know now exactly when our first kiss will be and how wonderful that day will be, spending time with him.

We talked and talked about just everything for another 20 minutes or so…about school, what our classes were for next year and whether we would be in many classes together besides Yearbook; obviously, we'll both be in that together seventh period, but I won't be in his remedial math class...about our jobs for next week, and about expanding our L&M business and how much money we could make this coming summer ...just everything. Then we realized that we barely had time to get home before dark, and it was time to go.

Last Week
of School

Chapter Fifty-Seven: Luke

This is the week school is finally over for the year, and on Monday Ms. Hawk asked Mia, Elly, and me to come in early before first period on Tuesday to talk about our duties for Yearbook next year and what she wanted us to do over the summer to get ready. I would never have believed before the school year started that a teacher would have called me in to talk to her, unless it was about my attitude sucking. But there I was sitting next to the two smartest, nicest girls in my class, and the teacher was treating us like we were equals...freaking unbelievable. Ms. Hawk told me to read plenty of sports stories over the summer, which I do all the time anyway, and to especially look for the action verbs that professional writers use ...that I had real potential as a professional writer myself. She asked had I thought about doing that? She said she knew that I really liked fishing and hunting a lot; would I write her a story about that over the summer and use a lot of action verbs and description and e-mail it to her for her to critique?

I told her I would write that story, that I had thought about becoming a professional writer a little, but more and more lately, I had thought about becoming a teacher. I told her Mia had sort of been putting a bug in my ear about that. I didn't tell her that one of the reasons that I was thinking about being a teacher was because I had had so many bad ones in middle school and already in high school. I've had too many teachers that just bore me and everybody else to death...those non-stop lectures like Mrs. Burkhead gives in biology and when those health teachers keep going on and on about the "wonders of the digestive system." Have some mercy on us, please!

I've been thinking about a lot of other things, too. In middle school, I didn't even think that I could stand high school enough to graduate and now I think I've definitely decided to go to college. I told Mom that, and she was really pleased, and she told me that no male in our family had ever graduated from high school and that my going on to college could give me a better life. She said she had been saving money for me to go…she had never told me that but I was really glad that she had been doing that. I don't want to touch my bank account money for college, I want to have it to buy some country land when I finish school, but I'll use it if I have to.

I wonder…I fear…that Mom would not be so pleased if she knew I am going to date a Hispanic girl next year. I know Dad would be furious about that, but I wouldn't listen to him, I definitely wouldn't follow his instructions if he forbade me from going out with Mia. But if I could get Mom on my side, maybe I could get away with Mia and me dating without Dad knowing. Should I talk to her about how wonderful Mia is? How smart she is and how she wants to become a nurse or maybe even a doctor? Mom knows my lawn mowing business has really picked up, but she doesn't know that it has happened because of Mia and me working together.

The other day Dad was talking again about how when I get my driver's license next year that I could go on weekend trips with him to buy used cars and drive them back home to our lot. I don't want to do that. I want to earn my own money for college or land doing my own business. I understand why Dad doesn't pay me to wash and wax his cars; those are my chores. But I don't want to go traveling around with him on weekends all over creation and picking up used cars. I worry that some of those cars might be hot, and if I got caught driving a hot car that I could get in trouble with the police. I don't want to be a part of his business.

Mia came up with another great idea for us to earn money with L&M during the winter months when lawns don't need mowing. She said we could have a lawn care arm of the business where we could "consult" with clients on how they could "enrich a garden" for wildlife. She said I already know what plants could be planted in a yard to draw birds and butterflies and that we could create the little plots in the winter and plant them in the spring and charge whatever is the going rate for that sort of thing...that we could "manicure," that was the word she used, the garden spot in the winter and plant in the spring.

The only worry that I had was who would trust two 15-year-olds to do such a job, and I told her that, and she said she would describe our services on the website and communicate with interested people by e-mail. If we got hired, then showed up to do the job, then our work would speak for itself. This girl is really smart. I don't know if this would work, but I know animals and plants and she knows gardening, so maybe it would work.

I want to try a little harder in school next year, so I can have a little better chance of getting into a college. I don't know what else I can do to score better in math. I am going to take Geometry next year. That course has got low *D* written all over it, even with Mia tutoring me. But I think I could make an *A* in history and maybe even in English 10 Honors. Ms. Hawk said she had two classes of that scheduled for her to teach next year, and maybe I could have her again. I couldn't stand her at first, but she's probably the best teacher I've ever had.

So if I can do a little better in school and go out with Mia, and if we could make good money at our business, life would be really good. And when I think of things that way, I get really hopeful about my future. But then I start to worry about my math grades dragging down everything next year, and Dad finding out about Mia and me dating and pitching a fit, and Dad making me go to car lots with him, and nobody hiring us very often to do jobs and then I get all worried and gloomy again. I guess I'll just to have to wait and see. It seems the older I get, the more complicated everything is.

Chapter Fifty-Eight: Elly

Right at the end of school, Ms. Hawk had Mia, Luke, and me come in to talk about how she plans to "take advantage of our skills" next year in Yearbook. She said I would be the photographer in charge of working with Luke in sports and Mia in features and that I would be going with them to take pictures. That sounds like a lot of fun. Dad has already said he would buy me a nice camera for my assignments, even though the Yearbook staff has several cameras I could use.

When I got to class early to meet with Ms. Hawk, Mia and Luke were already there and talking and laughing with each other. Ever since I figured out that Luke once had feelings for me, it's been on my mind, and I know this just sounds awful of me, but I finally have to admit that I'm jealous of Mia. But on the other hand, deep down, it's hard for me see myself with Luke. Dad would just hate it and probably get angry. But when I see Luke and Mia talking and laughing all the time and think of how Paul and I are together…boring… I just want more from a relationship.

My dream guy is still Caleb. We grew up in the same neighborhood, go to the same church, have had all kinds of classes together since grade school. He is so, so good looking and so athletic…and a sharp dresser, not that that is really important. Sometimes I dream of us being married and living in a house just like the ones in our neighborhood…how fantastic that would be.

Luke is so "earthy," that's the word, he seems so unconcerned about how he looks and whether he is making really good grades. He just seems content to make a *B* or a *C* in a subject, and I can't stand that attitude about grades. I made an *A* in every subject this year, and I knew I would; maybe I'm too obsessed with making great grades. The funny thing is that in English and history classes, Luke has spoken up and made comments about things for the first time since we've been going to school together. And what he says makes really good sense most of the time. He just doesn't seem to care about turning what he has learned into better grades.

Luke and Caleb are really different in how they look at things. If Caleb disagrees with someone in class, it's almost like he has contempt in his voice for that person, not just that person's ideas. On the other hand, Luke seems to respect other people's points of view and be sympathetic to the underdog. Maybe that's because of where his family lives. Luke never responds to somebody in a sarcastic tone.

Maybe if I went on a diet this summer, Caleb would notice me more when we went back to school. I would need to lose about 20 pounds, and I could also finally go through with my idea to let my hair grow longer. Of course, there's one more obstacle in my Caleb plan…Leigh, his current girlfriend. If you ask me, she's a little bit of an airhead and she wears her skirts way too short. Mary told me that she heard a rumor that Caleb and Marcus sometimes double date with two girls from Southside. I know that Marcus has been dating this girl named Tameka; Mary (she knows everything about everybody; how does she do that) said Caleb has been dating this other girl for about two months, but Leigh still doesn't know, and nobody likes her enough to tell her about it. But if Caleb would cheat on Leigh, who he's supposed to be going with, he could easily cheat on me.

So maybe I shouldn't go after Caleb this fall. I don't especially want to spend the summer dieting. Growing out my hair wouldn't be hard, except next fall it would take longer to take care of in the morning. But boys like girls with long hair, that's for sure. I don't think Caleb would cheat on me, since we've known each other so long. Why am I speculating about all this stuff? If I lose weight, if I grow my hair longer, if Caleb breaks up with Leigh, if I flirt with him enough for him to get interested in me, if he would be faithful to me. Why must I make a big deal about everything and overanalyze everything.

I think I'm going to be too busy this summer to go after Caleb and to diet. Dad's home office is at the beach. We're going to go down there for two weeks as soon as school lets out and stay at a really swanky cottage that Dad's company is paying for us to stay at. The first week down there, Dad won't be able to join us during the day; the second week, Dad says he will be on vacation and will be able to do family things with us. Two weeks at the beach should give me a lot of time to work on my tan and come back to school looking really good. But tanning is bad for you, so maybe I shouldn't do that and maybe I should try to cover up while I'm at the beach. Nobody wants to see a chunky girl waddling around in a bikini anyway. Maybe I'll meet this really hot guy at the beach and have a summer beach romance like in those romance novels, and we'll stay in touch afterwards and...there I go again.

After that, we will come home, and I will just have two days before I have to leave for a science and technology camp for advanced students that will last two weeks. Mom said she wants me to have plenty of options when it comes time to choose a career. She says the tech field pays really well. Mom knows I want to be a teacher, but she says teachers don't make a lot of money. I still think I want to teach little kids, though.

After that, I'll be home for only a week before we're going to go on a two-week tour of the West and visit, like, six states. I haven't really paid too much attention to what Mom and Dad have planned for that, it just seems so far off. I can work on my photography skills when I'm out West. I should be able to get some really neat photos. I'm going to love being on the Yearbook staff and doing things with Mia and Luke.

Chapter Fifty-Nine: Marcus

I'm in big trouble with my parents and Coach Dell. We had our nine weeks test in history Monday, and I calculated that if I got an A on the test, it would bring me up to a low B for the year, and I could tell Mom and Dad that I had brought my grades up in everything and they would stay off my back over the summer. So I made this great cheat sheet organized by the time periods that were going to be on the test and took a picture of it with my phone, and I figured that I could hide the phone between my legs and look down there when I needed to during the test.

But Mr. Foster busted me right at the beginning of the test. Foster walked up to me and said "Stand up," and I said no, I needed to work on the test, and then he was really rude and angry and said "Get up, now!" and I started to reach down and sort of slide my phone into a pants pocket, and he got up all in my face again and told me to leave my hands where they were. I got up and the phone fell on the floor, and everybody in class looked at me and Mary even snickered. Did she snitch on me …somebody must have…that's the first thing I thought. But then Foster said he had been watching me the past couple of tests and said I had been staring at my crotch area way too much. Then he picked up my phone and scrolled down the cheat sheet and said, "If you had spent as much time studying as you did making the cheat sheet, you wouldn't have needed the cheat sheet."

I can't stand it when a teacher gets sarcastic with me, and I started to say something right back to him, but then I realized I was in enough trouble as it was and why make things worse. Foster told me to follow him to his desk and he filled out a discipline referral form, and I didn't even have to look at it, I knew what he had written. It's the only time I've been written up all year. Coach Dell has told us over and over if we ever get written up that there will be "severe consequences" and Coach Henson has said pretty much the same thing. Foster wasn't content just to send me to the office...no, not him, the SOB has had in it for me since the first day of class. He told me he was going to call my parents during his planning period, that the test grade was one-third of my grade for the nine weeks, which meant that I would fail for the nine weeks and probably have a *D* for the year. So now I've gone from having a *B* for the year to probably having a *D*, all because of a jerk teacher.

And things just got worse from then on out. During lunch, Dad texted me and said he had had "an interesting conversation with your history teacher," and added that Mom and him would have "an interesting conversation" with me before dinner. His text was just nothing but pure sarcasm, he was acting like a child. Then during health seventh period, Coach Dell knocked on the door and said he wanted to speak to me, and he was all red in the face.

Dell told me as soon as we went out into the hall that my "conduct in history class was inexcusable" and that I was suspended from the football team for the first game this coming season. I told him that the suspension was unfair and that Foster had had it in for me all year, and before I even finished what I needed to say, Dell interrupted me and said that I was to address and refer to my history teacher as "Mr. Foster," that he had changed his mind and I was now suspended for the first two games and did I want "to keep running my mouth," and if so, then he could make the suspension three games long…that I had embarrassed the team and hurt the team's chances of winning with my actions…that all football players were representatives of the team in school and that he expected me to act like that in my grades and behavior. I started to say something right back to him, but I thought I had probably said enough already. He wasn't bluffing about suspending me for a third game, I could tell that.

Like two seconds after I got home, Mom and Dad got up in my face and told me that I was grounded for a month and that they were going to "rethink" their purchase of my new car. Then for the next ten minutes, they both took turns ranting at me. Mom was just as mad as Dad. I stopped listening after a while. Honestly, I was glad when they sent me to my room.

Joshua was waiting outside my door for me and then he lit into me, too. I told him to get out of my way and to shut up, that I had had enough crap from people today. He waited for me to pass him, then he took me by the arm and wrenched it around my back and slammed my face against the hall wall. I know Mom and Dad must have heard that noise, but they didn't do anything about it. Joshua had my left arm pinned against my back and with his other hand mashed my head against the wall and he told me I was to listen and to listen good!

He said Mom and Dad had worked really hard for us to have a really nice home and to live in an upper class neighborhood, that their parents had worked hard, too, and our great-grandparents had done the same, so all of us that came after them could have a better life. And that I "was disgracing their memory and disrespecting their sacrifices." I told him to shut up and he slammed me against the wall even harder, and, I swear, Mom and Dad must have known he was upstairs roughing me up and they didn't care.

Joshua was like seething with anger, and he told me to repeat after him every word he said, that I was "going to show more respect for Mom and Dad," and then he wrenched my arm and said repeat, and I said it, and then he said I was "going to show more respect for my teammates," and he yanked my arm again, and I begged him to stop, and he said, "stop begging and repeat after me," and I said it, and he said that I was "never going to cheat again," and I said yes, and he said did I need to be slammed up against the wall one more time just to make sure that I would remember all this, and I said no. And he slammed me up against the wall even harder and said "No what?" It took me a while to figure out that he meant for me to say no sir, and I didn't want to say it, but he was in such a rage that I was scared he was going to twist my arm off right there, so I said "No, sir."

"One last thing," he said. "All you are is one torn ACL from never playing high school football again or ever trying to play in college. You had better remember that and why your grades are so important."

Chapter Sixty: Mia

I came up with this great idea to help Luke and me make more money and get to spend more time with him this summer. We have four hens that are incubating about a dozen eggs each, and I told Mama and Poppa that Luke and I could build a second chicken coop as soon as school ended, and I would raise those 50 or so chicks as meat birds and sell them through my website as "fresh, unfrozen, organically raised chickens." Every time I made a sale, I could butcher a chicken and deliver it on my bike if the house was close enough or Mama could drive me there if it wasn't, and I would just add a shipping charge. Poppa said that was a fantastic idea, that he could ask his boss for leftover construction wood and other building material, and it wouldn't cost us anything to build the henhouse and run except for what I had to pay "the white boy working for me." That I could pay him either by the hour or, even better, out of some percentage of what I made selling the chickens. Mama said it was a great idea, too.

I was really glad that both my parents liked the idea, but then I realized that Poppa didn't understand that Luke and I are partners, that he probably thought the L in L&M in our business stood for lawn mowing or something like that instead of Luke. That one of the things that Poppa likes about my business is that a white boy is working for a Hispanic girl.

Wednesday, since school is out for the summer at the end of this week, Luke rode the bus home with me so we could work on the henhouse. He said he could jog home after we were finished for the day. We got a lot of work done before Mama and Poppa came home from work, and I was really excited (but a little worried, too) about Poppa meeting Luke. I so want Poppa to see what a nice boy Luke is. When they got home, Mama came over and said hi to Luke and me and said it was good to see him again and she complimented us on how much we had already gotten done. But Poppa didn't say anything to anybody and just went on in the house.

I had told Luke he could eat dinner with us, and he said that would be great, and I so much wanted Poppa to see how smart he is and how polite. But when dinnertime came, Poppa came out and told me it was time for dinner and to come inside and added that "Mia's mama will be bringing you a sandwich and something to drink" to Luke and for him "to keep on working." It was so rude, and I was both mad and embarrassed and really hurt and I almost started to cry, I was so shocked at Poppa's behavior. But I held back my tears because things were awkward enough, so I just came on inside.

When I got inside, Mama was starting to serve dinner and she asked where Luke was. Poppa interrupted her and said the white boy was going to eat outside with the chickens. Mama said that was rude, and Poppa disagreed and told her to go bring the boy a sandwich. Mama said she would not, she was going to tell him to come inside; and Poppa got up and slammed the table, got some peanut butter out of the pantry and spooned a gob of it between two pieces of bread, filled up a glass of water, and stormed out of the kitchen. When he got back, nobody said anything during dinner, not even my sisters—they could tell something was wrong and knew not to mess with Poppa. I tried to eat my dinner really fast, but I had been holding back tears for so long, that I started to cry a little, then I just started sobbing...I couldn't help it.

When I got myself together, I asked to be excused from the table and Poppa nodded, and I went to the bathroom to dry my eyes and compose myself so that Luke wouldn't know I had been crying. I didn't know what to tell him about the dinner, but he was so sweet when I came out; he said to thank my parents for the sandwich and to tell them that he appreciated it. We worked for about two more hours, then it started to get dark and Luke said he had better leave to jog home and that we could work again on Friday when we got out early on the last day of school. I walked over to him and squeezed his hand, and he squeezed back and left. He knew something was up with my poppa's behavior, but he just played it off. He was so sweet and kind to me to do that.

When I got inside, Mama and Poppa were sitting in our living room and neither one was talking and they both had angry expressions on their faces. I told them that Luke, (and I used his name, I wanted Poppa to at least know what his name was, that he just wasn't "the white boy,") had said to tell them thank you for the sandwich, that he appreciated it. I then said I was going to take a bath and go to bed, I was tired. I started to cry again, but I stopped myself from tearing up in front of Poppa.

When I got out of the bathroom, I could hear Mama and Poppa arguing. They almost never argue and when they do it is very quiet and very short. But this time, Mama was really angry, and her voice was louder than Poppa's and he was pretty loud, too. I felt bad that I had caused them to argue, but this wasn't my fault. Poppa behaved in a shameful way. After they finished arguing, Mama came to my room and asked if I was asleep, and of course I said no, and she apologized for Poppa's behavior. She said that she liked Luke and that she preferred that I go out with a Hispanic boy next year when I could date, but if Luke was the boy I wanted to go out with, she would be okay with that...that I had to make my own decisions about those things, and she knew that I would never let her down. I thanked and thanked Mama and hugged her so hard. And then I said that I had a confession to make, that Luke and I had already planned our first date when school started in August, that we were going to go on a picnic when the first Saturday came.

The next day after school, when Mama and Poppa came home from work, I was out working on the henhouse, doing some simple odds and ends. Poppa came over to me and asked if I knew that he worked on the construction gang with Ricardo's father, "you know, the family that lives several blocks down the street," the same family that goes to mass with us. I said yes, and Poppa said that Ricardo's poppa had said Ricardo (he's a rising senior at my school) had asked about me and said he had been thinking about asking me out next year when school started back up, and I was old enough to date. I told Poppa that Ricardo wasn't "my type," and Poppa said, "We'll see about that," and turned around and left.

I don't want to ever disobey my parents, but I wouldn't be disobeying Mama when I go out with Luke next year. I don't know how this is going to turn out.

# # #

ABOUT THE AUTHOR

Bruce Ingram is a high-school English teacher and lifelong outdoorsman who has written five well-reviewed river guides set in his native Virginia. He and his wife Elaine have also written the *Living the Locavore Lifestyle,* a guide to more sustainable and healthy living based on hunting, fishing, gathering, and gardening. *Ninth Grade Blues* is his first novel. Look for the sequel, *Tenth Grade Angst,* in 2018.

Made in the USA
Middletown, DE
12 September 2018